WEIRD ROMANCE

Two One-Act Musicals of Speculative Fiction

Music by **ALAN MENKEN**
Lyrics by **DAVID SPENCER**

"The Girl Who Was Plugged In"
Book by **ALAN BRENNERT** and **DAVID SPENCER**
based on the story by James Tiptree, Jr.

"Her Pilgrim Soul"
Book by **ALAN BRENNERT**
based on his original story

SAMUEL FRENCH, INC.
45 West 25th Street NEW YORK 10010
7623 Sunset Boulevard HOLLYWOOD 90046
LONDON *TORONTO*

Amateurs wishing to arrange for the production of WEIRD ROMANCE must make application to SAMUEL FRENCH, INC., at 45 West 25th Street, New York, NY 10010, giving the following particulars:

(1) The name of the town and theatre or hall of the proposed production.
(2) The maximum seating capacity of the theatre or hall.
(3) Scale of ticket prices.
(4) The number of performances intended and the dates thereof.
(5) Indicate whether you will use an orchestration or simply a piano.

Upon receipt of these particulars SAMUEL FRENCH, INC., will quote terms and availability.

Stock royalty quoted on application to SAMUEL FRENCH, INC., 45 West 25th Street, New York, NY 10010.

For all other rights than those stipulated above, apply to The Shukat Company, Ltd., 340 West 55th Street, Ste 1A, New York, NY 10019 on behalf of David Spencer and Alan Menken and to International Creative Management, Inc. on behalf of Alan Brennert.

An orchestration consisting of:

Keyboard/Conductor Score
Keyboard II
Bass
Percussion

will be loaned two months prior to the production ONLY on receipt of the royalty quoted for all performances, the rental fee and a refundable deposit. The deposit will be refunded on the safe return to SAMUEL FRENCH, INC. of all materials loaned for the production.

Printed in the U.S.A.
ISBN 0 573 68136 8

Notes by David Spencer

IMPORTANT BILLING AND CREDIT REQUIREMENTS

All producers of WEIRD ROMANCE *must* give credit to the Authors of the Work in all programs distributed in connection with performances of the Work, and in all instances in which the title of the Work appears for the purposes of advertising, publicizing or otherwise exploiting a production thereof; including, without limitation, to programs, souvenir books and playbills. The names of the Authors *must* also appear on a separate line in which no other matter appears, immediately following the title of the Work, and *must* be in size of type not less than 50% of the size of type used for the title of the Work. Billing *must* be substantially as follows:

(Name of Producer)
presents

WEIRD ROMANCE
Two One-Act Musicals of Speculative Fiction

Music by ALAN MENKEN
Lyrics by DAVID SPENCER

"The Girl Who Was Plugged in"
Book by ALAN BRENNERT and DAVID SPENCER
based on the story by James Tiptree, Jr.

"Her Pilgrim Soul"
Book by ALAN BRENNERT
based on his original story

Producers shall accord the following billing credit (in size not less than 25% of the size of the non-artwork title of the play as it appears in all programs, advertising, etc., in connection with all productions of the play:

"Originally produced by the WPA Theatre, New York City, Kyle Renick, Artistic Director."

To the actors, musicians and writers
who worked so hard
to make this musical a reality.

—Alan Menken

With undying gratitude,
to the members of the One Sixteenth Club:
MICHAEL LEEDS
NANCY GOLLADAY
and DENIS MARKELL;
and with undying love,
as ever,
to JOAN

—David Spencer

For IAN, LISA, and JILL:
Your mother's spirit lives in this play
even as she lives in you.

And for ALICE SHELDON,
a.k.a. James Tiptree, Jr.,
whose spirit also lives herein

—Alan Brennert

MUSICAL NUMBERS

Act I: "THE GIRL WHO WAS PLUGGED IN"

"Weird Romance"	Shannara & Zanth
"Stop and See Me"	P. Burke
"That's Where We Come In"	Isham, P. Burke, and Technicians
"Feeling No Pain"	Delphi, Joe
"Pop! Flash!"	Handlers, Delphi, Isham, Joe and Reporter(s)
"Amazing Penetration"	Isham and Female Assistants
"Eyes That Never Lie"	Paul
"No One Can Do"	Joe and P. Burke
"Worth It"	Delphi and P. Burke
"Eyes That Never Lie" (Reprise)	Paul
Final GTX Sequence:	
"Weird Romance" motif	Zanth & Shannara
"Stop and See Me"	Delphi and P. Burke
"Weird Romance" (Act I Finale)	Zanth & Shannara

Act II: "HER PILGRIM SOUL"

Opening Sequence:	
"Weird Romance" motif	Disembodied Female Voice
"I Can Show You a Thing or Two"	Johnny Beaumont
"Happy in Your Work"	Daniel
"My Orderly World"	Kevin
"My Orderly World" (fragment)	Carol
"Need to Know"	Daniel
"You Remember"	Kevin, Nola and Daniel
"You Remember" (Part II)	Kevin and Nola
"Another Woman"	Carol and Kevin
"Pressing Onward, Moving Forward"	Nola, Susan, Chuck, Kevin, Lester and Daniel
"I Can Show You a Thing or Two"	Johnny Beaumont
"A Man"	Rebecca and Carol
"Pressing Onward, Moving Forward" (Reprise)	Ruskin
"Someone Else is Waiting"	Nola and Kevin
"I Can Show You a Thing or Two"(Act II Finale)	Johnny Beaumont

CHARACTERS

Note: the assigning of multiple roles may vary from production to production of *Weird Romance*. The breakdown below reflects only the original New York production. For example, while an older Kevin (in Act II) may double as Isham (in Act I), a younger Kevin [which is, in some ways, even more ideal] may double as Joe; the actor playing Isham might subsequently double as Ruskin, etc. It is also possible [and again, possibly even ideal] to configure the casting such that no actor plays a lead role in both plays; so that the ensemble of each becomes the lead players in the other. And the cast need not be limited to nine.

Act I: "THE GIRL WHO WAS PLUGGED IN"

SHANNARA (Actress #1)
ZANTH (Actor #1)
FANS (Actress #2, Actress #3, Actor #2)
ISHAM (Actor #3)
PAUL (Actor #4)
P. BURKE (Actress #4)
MUGGER (Actress #2)
PARAMEDICS (Actors #1 & #2)
JOE (Actor # 5)
DELPHI (Actress #3)
TECHNICIANS (Actresses #1 & #2, Actors #1 & 2)
MOVEMENT COACH (Actor #1)
DIALOGUE COACH (Actress #2)
MAKE-UP SPECIALIST (Actress #1)
REPORTERS (Actor #2)
ISHAM'S ASSISTANTS (Actresses #1 & #2)
DIRECTOR (Actor #2)

Act II: "HER PILGRIM SOUL"

JOHNNY BEAUMONT [hologram] (Actor #4)
DANIEL GADDIS (Actor #2)
KEVIN DRAYTON (Actor #3)
BOXER [hologram] (Actor #1)
BRIDE [hologram] (Actress #3)
CAROL DRAYTON (Actress #2)
REBECCA (Actress #1)
NOLA (Actress #4)
SUSAN GRANVILLE (Actress #3)
CHUCK (Actor #5)
LESTER (Actor #1)
RUSKIN (Actor #5)

For BILL — the wonderfulness of yourself, sir — and DONNA from tie-in mania East — aka David Spencer 3/3/95

A NOTE ABOUT THE PLAY

Weird Romance takes its speculative fiction seriously. It is never to satirize the genre or degenerate into camp.

The first act ("The Girl Who Was Plugged In") satirizes a social condition, but again, not SF as a category. In re: the satire — though the ancillary characters may be taken to *tasteful* extremes, the central characters should remain "grounded." The story is best thought of as a combination of an edgy industrial and a black-and-white morality play, not unlike an old *Twilight Zone* episode in its intent. Futurism in the physical production is not so important as what might be accomplished via *suggestion,* through tricks of light, shadow and performance values. The future the tale projects is not so terribly far removed from our own and shouldn't be made exotic so much as pointed. It represents the next logical extension of current commercial-minded absurdities. To paraphrase SF writer Bernard Wolfe: Speculative fiction writers don't truly write about the future; they write about what the present might be like if it went on forever ...

The second act ("Her Pilgrim Soul") needs little in the way of advisories. In terms of character behavior, strive for truth, simplicity and verisimilitude. If you're honest with the story, it will reward you handsomely.

For the production team (director, designers, etc.), it bears to keep in mind that *Weird Romance* has a larger agenda than just accurate musical theatre treatment of SF. It means to use SF as a way of exploring two sides of love and what drives the emotion. Act I concentrates on the externals, and the folly of their worship. Act II is concerned with an *inner* journey, and is meant, of course, to represent the truer path.

"Weird Romance" opened June 14, 1992 at the WPA Theatre in New York City (Kyle Renick, Artistic Director). It was directed by Barry Harman and choreographed by John Carrafa. The musical direction and vocal arrangements were by Kathy Sommer, the orchestrations and synthesizer programming by Douglas Besterman. The settings were by Edward T. Gianfrancesco, the lighting by Craig Evans, the costumes by Michael Krass, and the sound by Aural Fixation. The casting was by Stephanie Klapper and the Production Stage Manager was Joseph A. Onorato.The cast played multiple roles as follows (lead roles are in bold print; roles from *The Girl Who Was Plugged In* are in plain type; roles from *Her Pilgrim Soul* are in italics; performers are numbered, and their roles listed, in order of appearance):

Danny Burstein (Actor #2)
[Third Fan, Second Paramedic, Technician, Reporters, Director, ***Daniel Gaddis***]

Ellen Greene (Acress #4)
[**P. Burke**, ***Nola***]

Jonathan Hadary (Actor #3)
[**Isham**, ***Kevin Drayton***]

Marguerite MacIntyre (Actress #3)
[First Fan, **Delphi**, *Susan Granville*]

Jessica Molaskey (Actress #2)
[Second Fan, Mugger, Voice Coach, ***Carol Drayton***]

Valarie Pettiford (Actress #1)
[**Shannara**, Technician, Make-up Specialist, ***Rebecca***]

(cont.)

Eric Riley (Actor #1)
[**Zanth,** First Paramedic, Technician, Movement Coach, *George Lester*]

Sal Viviano (Actor #5)
[**Paul,** *Johnny Beaumont*]

William Youmans (Actor #6)
[**Joe Hopkins,** *Chuck, John Ruskin*]

Prologue & Scene 1

(In BLACKNESS, we hear an ANNOUNCER's voice.)

ANNOUNCER. Ladies and gentlemen, welcome to the GTX Colosseum ... And now, get ready for the singing sensations of the Twenty-first Century. The "GTX in Concert" series — in association with GTX Enterprises — proudly presents ... *Zanth* and Shan*nara*!

[MUSIC CUE #1: WEIRD ROMANCE]

(LIGHTS up on a futuristic concert stage as ZANTH and SHANNARA make a flashy entrance.)

SHANNARA.
WHAT DOES THE FUTURE HOLD?
WHAT CAN IT HOLD WITH STRANGE, UNLIKELY LOVERS?
BREAKIN' THE NORMAL MOLD,
EASY ENOUGH TO PICTURE UNDER COVERS:
PRETTY AND PERFECT OUTSIDE ...
BUT WHEN YOU LOOK WITHIN —
THIS IS A WEIRD ROMANCE!
THIS IS A WEIRD ROMANCE!
IT'LL BE WEIRD ROMANCE
WHEN THEY BEGIN.
ZANTH.
WHAT'LL TOMORROW BRING?
WHAT CAN IT BRING WHEN LOVERS ARE CONNECTING?
SHOULD BE A LONG-TERM THING,
SAVE FOR THE ONE DETAIL WE'RE ALL NEGLECTING:
MAYBE THEY MATCH UP INSIDE ...

BUT WHEN YOU LOOK WITHOUT —
THIS IS A WEIRD ROMANCE!
THIS IS A WEIRD ROMANCE!
PERFECTLY WEIRD ROMANCE …

SHANNARA & ZANTH.
TELL US, O, STARS ABOVE:
IS IT A BRAVE, NEW LOVE?
OR IS IT JUST SO WEIRD
YOU HAVE TO DOUBT?

(During the instrumental break, we discover ISHAM and PAUL watching the proceedings on a monitor backstage. As the dialogue continues, three rabid FANS watch ZANTH and SHANNARA adoringly.)

ISHAM. (*Consulting a clipboard.*) Okay, has he gone for the XTC Cola yet?

(ZANTH produces a can of cola, sips.
All three FANS dutifully produce their own cans and sip.)

PAUL. Cola, check.

ISHAM. Next should be the Laser Light 200s.

(SHANNARA produces a pack of green cigarettes, tokes one. THE FANS produce their own and follow suit.)

PAUL. Cigarettes, check.

ISHAM. Mercatti body lift bracelets.

PAUL. Uh-oh.

ISHAM. What do you mean uh-oh. (*Looks up at the screen.*) Where are the body-lifts? Where the hell are the body-lifts?

PAUL. I … I don't understand. I left them in their dressing rooms.

ISHAM. Paul, it was your responsibility to slip them on personally! Give me one good reason why I shouldn't fire you.

PAUL. (*Long suffering.*) I don't know, Dad.

ISHAM. This isn't funny! How will the public know what to buy if the talent doesn't show them. Who would have thought the Federal Government would pass a law making advertising illegal? It's like outlawing *happiness*!

PAUL. Godssake, they were only commercials!

ISHAM. Don't start with me, Paul. Go out into the house, see how much damage they've done.

PAUL. Think I can handle it?

ISHAM. Go!

(PAUL, unhappily, runs off as:)

ZANTH.
SOMETHING UNKNOWN ...
SHANNARA.
OUT OF CONTROL ...
ZANTH.
SOMETHING THAT'S GROWN ...
SHANNARA.
OUT OF THE SOUL ...
ZANTH.
THE SCENARIO'S DANGER,
HOWEVER IT'S PLAYED ...
SHANNARA.
BUT THE PLAYERS KEEP ON PLAYIN'
LIKE THEY'RE NEVER AFRAID.
ZANTH.
DOESN'T MATTER WHAT'CHA TELL 'EM,
DOESN'T MATTER WHAT'CHA KNOW —
BOTH.
WITH A MATTER/ANTI-MATTER MATTER
THINGS ARE GONNA GO THE WAY THEY
GO IN A WEIRD ROMANCE!
TAKIN' THE WEIRDEST CHANCE!

WILL IT BE BURNING OUT
OR BURNING BRIGHT ... ?

ZANTH, SHANNARA, FANS.
WHEN IT'S A WEIRD ROMANCE?
AIN'T IT A WEIRD ROMANCE?
WE GOT A WEIRD ROMANCE
TONIGHT!

(The FANS disperse. ZANTH and SHANNARA are now backstage. Accosted by ISHAM:)

ISHAM. I thought you two were supposed to be wearing Mercatti body-lifts out there! What the hell is GTX paying you for anyway?

ZANTH. We've been having these, uhh ... what you call, "memory lapses," babe —

SHANNARA. Doctor says it's treatable but ... it's gonna cost big.

ISHAM. How big?

ZANTH. Well, health care today is just impossible.

ISHAM. *(A very loud silence. Then:)* Never let it be said that GTX doesn't care for the health of its employees. Will two thousand a week cover it?

SHANNARA. Three.

ISHAM. Done.

(PAUL re-enters, hanging back as:)

SHANNARA. (*Exiting, with a smile.*) I think my memory's improving already. *Ciao,* Paul.

ZANTH. (*Following; also to PAUL.*) See that the cola's chilled next time, willya, babe?

PAUL. Are you giving them another raise?

ISHAM. Consider it a flower for their Pyrrhic Victory garden. Let them enjoy it ... while they last. What've you got?

PAUL. I did the audience survey. Pretty much as you expected. Doesn't matter that you *tell* 'em Zanth wears a body-lift, they've got to see to believe.

ISHAM. Naturally. Well, they'll be wearing them at the reception at least. Maybe we can get some ink out of this fiasco. Call the Media Department. (*HE starts to exit as:*)

PAUL. You know, we're not curing ozone sickness here. It's only a lousy product.

ISHAM. "A lousy product"? There is no such thing as "a lousy product." The public attains its identity through these products. What you choose to wear and buy is *what you are*! Not curing ozone sickness? We are doing far more than that, my son —

PAUL and ISHAM. *We are defining the character of a nation!*

ISHAM. (*A beat.*) Besides, that lousy product pays your salary.

(JOE HOPKINS, a technician, enters, looking flustered.)

JOE. Uh, Mr. Isham, sir, there's a problem with …

ISHAM. (*ISHAM holds up a hand; this conversation will not be for his son's ears.*) Just a moment, Hopkins. (*To PAUL.*) Now, if you want to learn the business, you do it my way. What'll it be, Paul?

PAUL. (*Defeated.*) I'll call the goddamn Media Department. *(HE exits.)*

ISHAM. Hopkins —

JOE. — yessir —

ISHAM. — don't ever have children —

JOE. — nossir.

ISHAM. Speaking of which, I told you, my son has not been cleared to know about the project. He has to prove himself first.

JOE. I'm sorry, sir, but I thought you'd want to know as soon as possible, the last test subject didn't work out.

[MUSIC CUE #1B: ISHAM IS NOT HAPPY]

ISHAM. That's unacceptable, Hopkins. Why didn't she work out?

JOE. Her ego imperative was too strong.

ISHAM. Her *what*?

JOE. Let me put it this way. She had too much self-esteem.

ISHAM. Hopkins, I've built an empire on an entire *public* that has no self-esteem. Put out the word in the free-lance sector if necessary. That woman exists somewhere and *I will have her found.*

[MUSIC CUE #1C: BURKE ENTERS]

(THEY exit as, outside the theatre, P. BURKE, a bag lady, sad but somehow soulful, enters. TWO FANS, a couple holding hands, pass by her and SHE attempts to panhandle.)

FIRST FAN. You know, Zanth is much shorter in real life.

SECOND FAN. Yeah, but I love *her*!

P. BURKE. Excuse me, I'm hungry, could you spare some —

FIRST FAN. Boy, did you catch that smell?

SECOND FAN. I am so tired of people asking me for money.

(P. BURKE collects her bags, no stranger to this kind of defeat, and moves downstage.)

[MUSIC CUE # 2: STOP AND SEE ME]

P. BURKE.

NOT THAT I MIND THE STREET …
LIVE HOW I GOTTA LIVE …

THING THAT I MIND
AFTER YEARS OF THE GRIND
IS I'M STILL A BIT SENSITIVE.
SILLY ME BUT I WISH, AS FOLKS WALK BY,
THEY'D STOP … AND SEE ME.
SAY "HI."

SOMETIMES I CATCH A GLANCE.
CONTACT IS ALL TOO BRIEF.
EYES DART ASIDE LIKE THEY'RE WANTING TO HIDE,
JUST AS GUILTY AS ANY THIEF.
HEY, NO CAUSE FOR ALARM, NO NEED TO STAY…
JUST STOP … AND SEE ME.
OKAY …?

ONCE UPON A WISH,
I'D'VE WISHED THAT LIFE WERE FAIR;
ONCE UPON A WISH,
I'D'VE WISHED FOR NO MORE FEAR;
ONCE UPON A WISH,
I'D'VE WISHED FOR ONE MORE CHANCE.
NOW I ONLY WISH
I WOULDN'T DISAPPEAR.

ONE THING ABOUT THE STREET:
USED TO A LOTTA STUFF.
OTHERS I'VE SEEN, IT'S TOO MUCH OR TOO MEAN,
AND THEY DIE WHEN THEY'VE HAD ENOUGH.
ME, WHATEVER, I GO THAT EXTRA MILE
CUZ SOMEDAY SOMEONE …
DON'T KNOW — JUST … *SOMEONE* …
MIGHT STOP … AND SEE ME.
AND SMILE.

(The song buttons. [MUSIC CUE #2A: SPARE CHANGE] A FIGURE IN A ROBE appears. P. BURKE approaches with her bags.)

P. BURKE. Excuse me, can you spare some change?

(The FIGURE turns.)

P. BURKE. (*Beseechingly.*) I'm hungry.

(THE FIGURE beckons her over.)

P. BURKE. Oh, thank you, thank you so much, I—

[MUSIC CUE #2B: THE MUGGER]

(But this has been a ruse to catch her off-guard. As soon as P. BURKE approaches, the FIGURE assaults her and steals her bags, running off ... leaving P. BURKE, hurt and unconscious, center stage. Segue into:)

Scene 2

(Sound of a SIREN as two PARAMEDICS take position on either side of P. BURKE in a moving ambulance.)

FIRST PARAMEDIC. Dammit. I'm missing *Autopsies of the Rich and Famous*.

SECOND PARAMEDIC. Geez, did you see what they did to Regis and Kathie Lee last week?

FIRST PARAMEDIC. That's nothing. Tonight they're doin' Oprah.

SECOND PARAMEDIC. I heard. It's supposed to be a two-parter.

FIRST PARAMEDIC. Think we'll get back before it's over?

SECOND PARAMEDIC. (*Re: their patient.*) I don't know, she's in pretty shitty shape.

FIRST PARAMEDIC. Oh, great. She kacks on us we'll be filling out forms the whole goddamn night.

SECOND PARAMEDIC. So give me the frikkin' microchip, willya? (*Presses a blunt-end hypo to her temple. It hisses.*) That may hold her … BP one hundred over seventy. (*Glances at a monitor.*) Hey-hoo. Check out the psych profile on this one!

FIRST PARAMEDIC. Son of a bitch. I haven't seen a Sublimation Index that low since — (*A beat.*) Helluva finder's fee if she works out.

SECOND PARAMEDIC. Forget the hospital?

FIRST PARAMEDIC. Damn straight. GTX'll want first crack at this one.

SECOND PARAMEDIC. What about Centex? They're lookin' for one of these too.

FIRST PARAMEDIC. Better deal from GTX. Trust me.

SECOND PARAMEDIC. GTX it is. (*To the comatose P. BURKE as HE prepares another hypo.*) Hey you. Don't die.

[MUSIC CUE #2C: LIFE OR DEATH]

(The hypo hisses again as the lights on the PARAMEDICS fade, leaving only P. BURKE illuminated. Through this:)

VOICE #1. — BP eighty over sixty —

VOICE #2. We're losing her! Cordrazine, twelve cc's, stat!

VOICE #1. BP seventy over fifty-five —

VOICE #3. (*Hiss of another hypo.*) Cordrazine, twelve cc's —

VOICE #1. Eighty over sixty-five and rising —

VOICE #3. Subject stabilizing —

(And the voices carry over to:)

Scene 3

(A hospital bed. P. BURKE lies unconscious. ISHAM appears with JOE.)

ISHAM. What's her prognosis, Hopkins?

JOE. All vital signs are stable, sir. We expect a complete recovery. She appears to be an excellent candidate for the program, self-esteem is definitely not a problem here ... assuming you're able to talk her into joining us.

ISHAM. I have some small powers of persuasion, Hopkins.

JOE. Yes, sir.

(JOE exits as P. BURKE stirs, sits up. ISHAM approaches.)

ISHAM. Ms. Burke? That is your name — (*HE consults her chart.*) P. Burke? (*SHE nods mutely.*) How are you feeling?

P. BURKE. They took everything I had.

ISHAM. (*Sympathetic.*) I know. I'm sorry. (*Produces a protein bar from his pocket.*) Here. Have some breakfast.

P. BURKE. (*Takes food greedily.*) Thank you, sir—

ISHAM. Interesting psych profile. You have some ... unusual talents.

P. BURKE. I do?

ISHAM. You certainly do. Where do you live?

P. BURKE. Sometimes I sleep under the freeway overpass. And when it's not too cold, I sleep on the beach.

ISHAM. (*A quick beat.*) Your family?

P. BURKE. Gone.

ISHAM. No job?

P. BURKE. Who'd hire me?

ISHAM. *I* might. Have you ever seen Shannara, Ms. Burke?

P. BURKE. Yes, sir. On the holo screens outside the colosseum, the day I was … hurt.

ISHAM. How would *you* like to be a star … just like her? Wear Mercatti clothes, like she does … eat at the Seventh Moon … live in a nice house … ?

P. BURKE. A house? Would it have a door? With a lock on it?

ISHAM. Two locks, if you wish.

P. BURKE. (*A beat. Tempted — then:*) You're making fun of me. (*SHE starts to move away, puts weight on her bad leg, winces.)*

ISHAM. How'd you like to get rid of that painful limp? (*That stops her.*) I can make it happen. Just work together with me and the staff here at GTX —

P. BURKE. GTX?

ISHAM. This isn't a hospital, Ms. Burke. You're in the research labs of the eighth largest industrial firm in America. This is our marketing division. (*A beat.)* Do you know what an … advertisement … is, Ms. Burke?

P. BURKE. (*Horrified.*) Something that … isn't allowed anymore, sir.

ISHAM. An irresponsible law. When it was put into effect, we had to find other ways to direct the public to our products. Celebrity endorsements seemed to be the answer. But … Celebrities — stars — are notoriously capricious. Difficult to control. And expensive. So at GTX … we're looking into ways … to grow our own.

[MUSIC CUE #3: THAT'S WHERE WE COME IN]

ISHAM.
WHAT MAKES A STAR?
IT WASN'T LONG AGO THAT NO ONE KNEW
BUT WITH TECHNOLOGY ADVANCING FAR ...
THERE'S NOW A SLIGHTLY DIF'RENT POINT OF VIEW—
SOME OF US DO:
A PERFECT SHELL,
A WILLING MIND,
ATTUNED TO EV'RY DEMOGRAPHIC NEED.
BUT, SAD TO TELL,
THE TWO COMBINED
ARE RARE INDEED,
AN ENDANGERED BREED.
AND SO, WITH NATURE INSUFFICIENT,
WE LET SCIENCE INTERCEDE.

THAT'S WHERE YOU COME IN.
YOU AND I.
HELPING OTHERS TO LEARN WHAT TO BUY.
I'LL PUT YOUR NAME
WITH A BRAND NAME
SO CONSUMERS WILL LINK YOU
WHEN ORDERING AND NAME
THE BRAND NAME YOU EXTOL,
SINCE TO EMULATE YOU IS THEIR GOAL —
CHOOSING, THUS, TO BE FREE
(THANKS TO YOU AND TO ME),
THEY FIND DESTINY THEIRS
TO RECLAIM AND CONTROL.

So you see, by coming to work for us, you'll actually be performing a valuable public service.

P. BURKE. But, sir, how could I possibly —

ISHAM. Oh, it's quite possible, Ms. Burke, *believe* me ... I want to show you something.

(A TECHNICIAN enters with a photo of a STUNNING BLONDE.)

P. BURKE. Oh. She's *beautiful* ...

ISHAM. She's meat.

P. BURKE. Excuse me?

ISHAM. Beautiful meat, granted, but — unthinking, unfeeling meat. Grown in a vat, a few cells shaved off a placenta, no one's the wiser. No mind. No soul. A simulacrum. Without an Operator, she's just a vegetable. You understand?

P. BURKE. Yes ... No.

ISHAM.
THAT'S WHERE YOU COME IN,
AND YOU BOND
WITH THIS EMPTY BUT INT'RESTING BLONDE;
FOR IMAGINE,
AS YOU SEE HER,
THAT IT'S YOURS FOR THE ASKING
TO ACTU'LLY BE HER —

P. BURKE. To ... to what?

ISHAM.
TO ACTU'LLY *BE* HER,
YOUR MIND MOVED FROM ITS PLACE
TO THIS FASH'NABLE CARRYING CASE.
JUST A FEW PALTRY WIRES
AND YOUR SECRET DESIRES
WILL BE WEARING, QUITE LITERALLY, A NEW FACE.

(Other TECHNICIANS appear.)

ISHAM. Well?

P. BURKE. Why me?

ISHAM. You're special, P. Burke.
MOST PEOPLE LAST, AT THE MOST, SEV'RAL HOURS.
WE NEEDED SOMEBODY DIF'RENT FROM MOST.

TECHNICIANS.
DIF'RENT FROM MOST!
ISHAM.
MOST PEOPLE COME WITH A STRONG SENSE OF SELF
AND REFLEXIVELY TEND TO REJECT THE NEW HOST.
TECHNICIANS.
CAN'T GET ENGROSSED.
ISHAM.
YOU, THOUGH, HAVE NO SUCH AUTONOMOUS POWERS,
NO SENSE OF SELF YOU MIGHT WISH TO PURSUE.
TECHNICIANS.
NONE TO PURSUE.
ISHAM.
YOU'RE IN SUCH PAIN, BOTH IN FLESH AND IN SPIRIT,
YOUR BODY PURSUES A REJECTION OF YOU.
TECHNICIANS.
YOU! YOU!
ISHAM and TECHNICIANS.
AND WOULDN'T YOU LOVE TO REJECT IT IN TURN?
ISHAM
TO JUST LET IT GO AND EMBARK ON A JOURNEY?
NO FEAR ...
NO CARE ...
(Taps her forehead.)
FROM HERE ...
(Indicates BLONDE.)
TO THERE ... ?
P. BURKE.
THERE ...
THERE ...
THERE ...

THERE ... WHERE *I* COME IN!

ISHAM.

AS I SAID.

P. BURKE.

THERE RIGHT THERE!

TECHNICIANS.

THERE RIGHT THERE!
IN THAT HEAD!

P. BURKE.

(Looks up quickly.)
WILL IT HURT?

ISHAM.

ON NO CONDITION.
SIMPLY MICROWAVES BEAMED
VIA RELAY TRANSMISSION
FROM YOUR BRAIN
INTO HERS.
INSTALLATION IS ALL THAT OCCURS.
THEN THE BEAMS CAN BE HURLED
ANYWHERE IN THE WORLD.

P. BURKE.

AND I RIDE ON THESE BEAMS?

ISHAM.

TO YOUR DREAMS!

P. BURKE.

TO MY —

ISHAM and TECHNICIANS.

AND THAT'S WHERE *SHE* COMES IN!

ISHAM.

LITHE AND BEAUTIFUL!
AND HER FANS —

P. BURKE.

I'LL HAVE FANS?

ISHAM.

AWED AND DUTIFUL.
AS YOU THROW THEM A BUFFET CRUMB,
EVEN YOU WON'T SUSPECT
SHE'S A MERE SIMULACRUM,

FOR, REVELLING IN THEIR CHEERS …

TECHNICIANS.

FERVENT CHEERS!

ISHAM.

YOU WILL HEAR THROUGH THOSE PEARL-PERFECT EARS.

TECHNICIANS.

SHELL-LIKE EARS!

P. BURKE.

WILL I FEEL THROUGH HER SKIN?

ISHAM.

EV'RY TEXTURE A FEAST!

P. BURKE.

WILL I SEE THROUGH HER EYES?

ISHAM.

TWENTY-TWENTY AT LEAST.

P. BURKE.

NO MORE PAIN?

ISHAM.

NO MORE PAIN.

P. BURKE

SHE'S AN ANGEL!

ISHAM and TECHNICIANS.

SHE WILL BE WITH YOU!

ISHAM.

THAT'S WHERE *WE* BEGIN ...

TECHNICIANS.

AND WHAT *SHE'S* ABOUT ...

ISHAM.

AND WHERE *YOU* COME IN ...

P. BURKE.

AND WHEN I COME *OUT*
I'LL BE NEW —

ISHAM and TECHNICIANS.

— BRAND —

P. BURKE.

BRAND

BOTH.
— NEW!

(Button. Over the above, P. BURKE has been cleaned up and led into a cyber-chamber upstage: large enough to accommodate a human being, with an array of technical equipment inside.)

P. BURKE. When do we … start?

[MUSIC CUE #3A: THAT'S WHERE WE COME IN PLAYOFF]

ISHAM. We already have. (*A short beat.*) P. Burke. What does the "P" stand for?

P. BURKE. Philadelphia.

ISHAM. Mmm. Philly. Liberty. Delphi … (*His imagination snared by that.*) Delphi … yes. Quite euphonious, don't you think? Shannara, Allura, Zanth … and now …

(TECHNICIANS turn around a second chamber and leave, revealing the unconscious and unaware BLONDE.)

ISHAM. Congratulations, Delphi, you're about to be born!

Scene 4

(Continuous, as JOE enters.)

ISHAM. There's someone I'd like you to meet. Joe Hopkins —

JOE. — Joe Hopkins, technical coordinator. It's an honor to meet you, Ms. Burke. I haven't seen a set of encephaloprints like yours since — well *ever,* actually. We're going to do great things together, Ms. Burke, great things.

P. BURKE. "Technical co-ordinator"?

ISHAM. Joe is one of the finest minds we have working at GTX.

JOE. (*Pooh-poohing; embarrassed.*) I designed the neural matrix. Everything from higher brain functions to fine motor controls …

ISHAM. I leave you in his capable hands. (*To JOE.*) I'll be watching on the monitor in my office. (*HE exits.*)

JOE. Anyway, yes, I designed the, uh … the cybernetic … mold … that will allow you to control, to … inhabit … *her.*

P. BURKE. How long do I have to be in here?

JOE. I know. Kind of claustrophobic, isn't it? But you've got to get *in* before you can get *out.* (*HE starts to close the chamber; SHE starts. Gently:*) Trust me. It's not going to hurt. It's the *end* of all hurt. The end of all pain. You ready? [MUSIC CUE #3B: I CAN'T I CAN] (*SHE nods; HE closes the doors.*) Comfortable?

P. BURKE. I guess.

JOE. Close your eyes. Can't have two sets of visual stimuli confusing you. Now think of — flying. *(HE hits a button. Machinery hums.*)

P. BURKE. I can't fly.

JOE. Yes you can. You can fly out of that body into a brand new one. You're the caterpillar, that's your cocoon, and you're about to become a brilliant, beautiful butterfly. Fly, Delphi, fly!

P. BURKE. I can't —

JOE. You can!

P. BURKE. I can't —

JOE. You can!

P. BURKE. I can't —

JOE. You can!

P. BURKE. I can't —

JOE. You *can*!

DELPHI. I *can't*!

(DELPHI has spoken, her eyes snapping open. JOE smiles.)

JOE. I think you just did.

(DELPHI's eyes close again; P. BURKE's open.)

JOE. How did it feel?
P. BURKE. Different …
JOE. Different, better?
P. BURKE. Different … I don't know. (*A moment of panic.*) I don't know, something felt wrong, I —
JOE. What, what's wrong? Nothing hurt, did it?
P. BURKE. No, it's not that, [MUSIC CUE #4: FEELING NO PAIN] it's — (*A beat. Then … awe.*) Wait. That's *exactly* what it is.
P. BURKE.
NOTHING HURTS.
THAT'S WHAT'S ODD.
"THE END OF ALL HURT..."
OH ... MY ...
DELPHI. (*Eyes snap open.*)
... GOD...

(P. BURKE looks out through DELPHI's wondering eyes as JOE rushes to her side.)

JOE. Hello. Have a nice trip? (*Helping her out of the chamber.*) Now the thing you have to realize is that body … Delphi … is like an infant's body. It's never walked. Try a step. (*SHE takes a step.*) It's never moved. Couldn't. There was nothing inside. So inhabiting it will be a little like your first ride on a bicycle. (*SHE slips, but HE catches her.*) We're going to have to work on the ambulatory thing. Try another step. (*SHE walks — with a limp.*) Wait a minute. Why are you limping?

DELPHI. I've always had a limp.

JOE. Not anymore. This leg bends. I should know, I designed it. (*HE inspects it.*) Try it. (*SHE does. Twice. Wonderingly:*)

DELPHI.
IMAGINE:
I HAVE TO
GET USED TO THE FACT
THAT I'M FEELING NO PAIN.
IMAGINE:
NOT KNOWING
THE RIGHT WAY TO ACT
CUZ I'M FEELING NO PAIN.
LIKE A PART OF ME REMOVED …
AND YET WITHOUT THE PART, IMPROVED.
SOMETHING NEW
I DON'T KNOW HOW TO USE

JOE.
SO GIVE YOURSELF SOME CLUES.
NOW —
(SHE tentatively starts moving.)
START MOVING …

DELPHI.
AND MOVING …
AND MOVING AGAIN, JOE.,
AND FEELING NO PAIN.

JOE.
NOW FLEXING —
AND STRETCHING —

DELPHI and JOE.
AND LIFTING AND BENDING —

DELPHI.
AND FEELING NO PAIN!
I COULD SPREAD MY WINGS
TO THEIR FURTHEST SPAN
AND I THINK I WILL,
JUST BECAUSE I CAN!
I'M FEELING NO PAIN!

FEELING NO PAIN!
FEELING —

(Dance as DELPHI gets used to her body into:)

JOE.
STOP THE PRESSES! START THE TAPING!
THE STORY AT ELEVEN IS DELPHI!
WHO'S THE STAR THEY'LL ALL BE APING?
A LITTLE BIT OF HEAVEN CALLED DELPHI!
DELPHI.
I FORECAST
WHAT'S COMING
THE REST OF MY DAYS:
NO PREDICTION OF RAIN.
JOE.
(WHO'S THE STAR IT DOESN'T RAIN ON?)
DELPHI.
ALL GOOSEFLESH
AND THRUMMING,
THE END OF A PHASE.
JOE.
KID, YOU GOT THROUGH THE PAIN —
DELPHI.
I'M LOOKIN' AT GAIN
AS AN ABSOLUTELY PERMANENT CONDITION.
A TECHNICIAN BROUGHT MY MISSION TO FRUITION!
OUT OF BODY, INTO BOD!
I'M NO LONGER —
(Giddily, SHE whips around — and sees, like a corpse in an open coffin, her old body in the cyber-cabinet.)
OH ... MY ... GOD!

JOE. Pay her no mind, Delphi, don't —

DELPHI. How — I mean, who — (*Spoken in alternation between her two selves:*) Which

P. BURKE. am

DELPHI. I,

P. BURKE. *who —*

JOE. (*Grabs her, turns her away, shakes her.*) *Stop* it! Somatic dissonance, that's all it is. You're *Delphi,* you understand? You're *Delphi*!

DELPHI. Delphi … ?

JOE. And perfect. (*Softly.*) I could work for another hundred years and never create anything as perfect as you. Look. (*HE turns her around to face her reflection.*)

DELPHI. (*Absolutely certain, now.*)
I'M DELPHI. …

BOTH.
AND I'M (YOU'RE) FEELING
NO PAIN!

BLACKOUT

Scene 5

(LIGHTS UP on ISHAM and PAUL.)

ISHAM. How difficult could it have been to get Astroboy Colodner's signature on a contract? He's an athlete, the only thing he knows how to *write* is his name!

PAUL. I wasn't dealing with him, I was dealing with his representation!

ISHAM. How can they outlaw advertising and not agents? All right. Get back on the phone and try again.

PAUL. I can't … He's already signed with Centex.

ISHAM. Can't you ever do —

PAUL. So I went and called Thundercat Roberts. It's off-season, he's free, we took a meeting — he's a lock.

ISHAM. (*Impressed, even pleased.*) Good! … Thundercat Roberts is old news, but good.

PAUL. Gee, thanks.

ISHAM. No, I mean it. Good initiative.

PAUL. Good enough to get some real responsibility for a change?

ISHAM. All ri-ight. I'm grooming a new star. A very *important* new star. Your job will be to make sure things go smoothly for her. Schedule her appointments, make sure she gets where she needs to be and does what she's supposed to do.

PAUL. (*Stung.*) In other words, I'm her baby sitter.

ISHAM. Call the job what you like. *I* call it what you asked for. (*And, as DELPHI. enters:*) And here's our baby now. Paul, this is Delphi. Delphi — (*PAUL exits, too angry to even nod at her.*) That was my son, Paul. Delphi, you look wonderful, how are you feeling?

DELPHI. Mr. Isham? I was just wondering … when do I get my door?

ISHAM. Your door? Oh, yes. Soon. But first, you must get ready for your training!

DELPHI. Training?

[MUSIC CUE #5: POP! FLASH!]

(DELPHI's HANDLERS appear: A MOVEMENT COACH, VOICE COACH and MAKE-UP SPECIALIST. ISHAM, an arm around her shoulders, gives her over to them.)

ISHAM. Your handlers … your teachers.

MAKE-UP SPECIALIST. Hello, Delph.

MOVEMENT COACH. Hiya, Delph.

VOICE COACH. Bon jour, Delphi.

ISHAM. They'll show you how to walk, how to talk, how to smile, how to laugh. (*On cue, the HANDLERS laugh. To HANDLERS.)* Take good care of her. (*HE exits.*)

DELPHI. I already know how to walk.

MOVEMENT COACH. No, you only think you do. Watch. (*Demonstrating the "proper" posture and walk. Rhythmic music under.*) Now you try.

DELPHI. (*It's not as easy as it looks.*) Can't I just walk like everybody else?

MOVEMENT COACH.
EV'RYONE ELSE
AIN'T A CELEB!
NOBODY WANTS YOU TO BE
EV'RYBODY ELSE, BABE;
WE GET THAT AT HOME!

WE WANNA BE
CAUGHT IN YER WEB!
IF WE CAN GET IT FOR FREE,
WE ARE NOT IMPRESSED, BABE:
MIGHT AS WELL GO HOME!

BUT WALK THE WALK,
AND IF YOU WALK IT PRETTY ...

POP! FLASH!
FREEZE FRAME!
WHO'S THAT?
THAT'S FAME!
BANG ZOOM!
MAKE ROOM!
YOU'RE A SMASH!
POP! FLASH!

(Crossing into another pool of light as the first one fades, DELPHI is handed a sheet of copy by the VOICE COACH.)

DELPHI. "Treyfallo designs my gowns. Isn't it the darlingest thing?"

VOICE COACH. More breath, less throat. Suggestive.

DELPHI. (*Gamely.*) "Treyfallo designs my gowns. Isn't it the darlingest —" (*A beat.*) I'm sorry, I feel silly. Will people really *believe* this?

VOICE COACH.
FANTASY, DEAR,
MUST BE SINCERE,
WHETHER OR NOT IT'S TRUE;
LONG AS YOU BELIEVE, DEAR,
WE BELIEVE IN YOU!

SO TALK THE TALK,
AND IF YOU TALK IT PRETTY ...
HANDLERS.
POP! FLASH!
FREEZE FRAME!
THEY SAW!
THEY CAME!
WHAM! BAM!
THANKS, MA'AM!
MADE A SPLASH!
POP! FLASH!

(Stepping into her own pool of light, DELPHI finds herself being made up by the MAKE-UP SPECIALIST; SHE wonders —)

DELPHI.
HERE IN THIS ROOM IT'S FANTASY …
HERE WHERE IT'S US AND JUST US …
WHAT MAKES YOU THINK *THEY'LL* GO FOR ME?
MOVEMENT COACH.
BABE —
VOICE COACH.
BABE —
MAKE-UP SPECIALIST.
BABE —
HANDLERS.
TRUST US!
MAKE-UP SPECIALIST. (*Other HANDLERS in back-up.*)
MANAGERS KNOW

HOW TO MAN-AHGE!
WE'RE GONNA GUIDE YOU TO SHORE!
PUBLIC DON'T REJECT YOU
WHEN YOU BRING IT HOME!

PACKAGING-WISE,
WHAT A PACK-AHGE!
BEEN THROUGH A BUSHEL BEFORE.
LET THE PROS DIRECT YOU ...
JUST RELAX THE DOME.
VOICE COACH.
THE WALK, THE TALK ...
MOVEMENT COACH.
KEY TO THE WHOLE DAMN CITY!
HANDLERS.
POP! FLASH!
FREEZE FRAME!
POW! ZAP!
NO SHAME!
STRAIGHT FLUSH!
HOT RUSH!
COLD CASH!
POP! FLASH!

(A short silence ... then, over the sound system — crowd NOISES. Reporters battling to be heard over one another. [NOTE: All the REPORTERS in this sequence can be played by the same actor.] A DRUMROLL. Cameras trained on ISHAM at a podium, speaking into a glass microphone.)

ISHAM. She was raised in a small midwestern town, the only daughter of humble silicone farmers. After an exhaustive search, she literally showed up on our front porch, and from the moment we saw her, we knew that she was truly — America's girl next door. Ladies and gentlemen — remember this moment. Someday, you'll be telling your sons, your daughters, that you were here, that you bore witness: that you were among the first to meet — Delphi!

(HE gestures grandly. A fanfare ... and DELPHI takes the spotlight as though born to it, flanked by her HANDLERS, who are now her backup chorus. SHE's been glamorized, looking every inch the stunning young starlet. Oohs and ahhs from the crowd.
The HANDLERS — joined by ISHAM and JOE — sing their paean ... DELPHI parading to it in regal style.)

HANDLERS.
DELPHI:
SHE'S WONDERFUL!
DELPHI:
SHE'S BEAUTIFUL!
SEXY
AND TALENTED TOO.
WHOLESOME,
LIKE STARS ON A COOL NIGHT.
NAUGHTY,
LIKE STAYING UP ON A SCHOOL NIGHT!

FIRST REPORTER. Ms. Delphi! Are you really from the Midwest?

(Her eyes dart from the reporter to ISHAM and back again. SHE's not sure SHE can pull it off. Another chord held ... then, a smile that could melt frozen methane and—)

DELPHI. Stubenville, Ohio.
HANDLERS.
DELPHI:
SO SINGULAR
WORDS ARE
SUPERFLUOUS;
MEET HER

AND SEE FOR YOURSELF IT'S TRULY TRUE!

SECOND REPORTER. What's your first role for GTX?

DELPHI. A contemporary version of *Our Town*, set on Jupiter's third moon. I play Emily, but instead of coming back from the dead I've been assimilated by an alien mass-mind, and I have to decide whether to take one last look at everyone I ever loved ... or eat them.

HANDLERS, et. al.
THOUGH SCHOLARS MAY YELL, "FIE!"
AND ARGUE THE NAME IS DELPH-EYE,
MYSELF, I DON'T THINK YOU'LL AGREE.
WHEN PICTURES OF DELPHI
GO UP ON YOUR SHELFIE,
YOU WILL PRONOUNCE DELPH-EYE
FOREVER
DELPH-EE!!!

(THEY all rush up to DELPHI, congratulating her, as LIGHTS CHANGE.)

ISHAM. And this is only the beginning, Delphi. How do you feel now?

DELPHI.
HOW DO I FEEL?
LIKE A CELEB.
LIKE A CELEB OUGHTTA FEEL!
LIKE IT'S ALL SO SIMPLE!
LIKE I NEVER FELT!

FOLLOWED THE PLAN,
SPUN 'EM A WEB.
GOD, IT WAS SO UNREAL!
ALL I DID WAS DIMPLE,
AND I SAW THEM MELT!

HANDLERS.
THAT'S WHAT'CHA GET
DOIN' IT BY COMMITTEE —

HANDLERS.
POP! FLASH!

THIRD REPORTER. Ms. Delphi, who designs your gowns?

DELPHI. Treyfallo designs my gowns — isn't it the darlingest thing?

HANDLERS.
POP! FLASH!

FOURTH REPORTER. Who does your hair?

DELPHI. The Mane Event. Antonio, I love you!

HANDLERS.
POP! FLASH!

FIFTH REPORTER. What's that scent you're wearing?

DELPHI. Morning Primrose. Isn't it divine?

HANDLERS.
POP! FLASH!

SIXTH REPORTER. Your skin is so clear, what's your beauty secret?

DELPHI. Six glasses of water a day, every day. And I only drink Crystal Springs.

HANDLERS.
THE WALK, THE TALK …
KEY TO THE WHOLE DAMN CITY.

ALL.
POP! FLASH!

MOVEMENT COACH.
(FREEZE FRAME!)

ALL.
CROWD ROARS!

MAKE-UP SPECIALIST.
(TAKE AIM!)

ALL.
SHE SHOOTS!

VOICE COACH.
(NO SHAME!)

ALL.
SHE SCORES!

VOICE COACH.
(THEY CAME!)
ALL.
STRAIGHT FLUSH!
MOVEMENT COACH.
(BIG NAME!)
ALL.
HOT RUSH!
VOCAL COACH & MAKE-UP SPECIALIST.
(THAT'S FAME!)
ALL.
COLD CASH!
POP! FLASH!

(Button. BLACKOUT.
[MUSIC CUE # 5A: THEY SAW ME]
A beat. And LIGHTS COME UP on P. BURKE as JOE helps her out of the cyber-chamber.)

P. BURKE. (*Wired; jazzed.*) Did you *see,* Joe? Did you see me?

JOE. (*Genuine affection.*) You were terrific, kiddo. You were perfect.

P. BURKE. (*Can hardly believe it.)* They were all looking at me. Not looking *away*. Looking at *me.*

JOE. And that's only the beginning. (*Leading her off.*) Delphi's body is sleeping ... time for you to exercise yours. After that we've got a nice dinner and a soft bed for you back here ...

P. BURKE. I can't ... sleep ... in there?

JOE. It's not a good idea to let your real body become too dependent on the chamber's life-support systems. But sixteen hours out of twenty-four ... that's still not bad, is it, Phil?

P. BURKE. Phil?

JOE. If you don't mind my being familiar. What do your friends call you?

P. BURKE. (*As THEY move offstage.*) I never — (*Then.*) I guess they call me Phil.

(*And as THEY exit, LIGHTS FADE.*)

[MUSIC CUE #5B: ISHAM INTRO]

Scene 6

(*ISHAM addresses an unseen board meeting flanked by two FEMALE ASSISTANTS at easels, flipping graphics as HE uses a pointer for emphasis.*)

ISHAM. Esteemed members of the Board of Directors. Our forays into Celebrity Sciences have left our competitors in the proverbial dust. It has been a mere six months since we've introduced Delphi to the public. And already the results have been — phenomenal, to say the least.

[MUSIC CUE #6: AMAZING PENETRATION]

WE'VE ACHIEVED AMAZING PENETRATION:
DELPHI HAS EXTRAORDINARY 'Q' LEVELS —
ON ALL THE STRATA.
I REFER YOU TO THE BOUND REPORT,
SPECIFIC'LLY THE DEMOGRAPHIC DATA.

NINETY-FIVE PERCENT OF WOMEN,
NINETY-TWO PERCENT OF MEN —
(AS OF JUNE, IT'S BOTH THE HETERO AND GAY SET).
AND SOME FIFTY MILLION CHILDREN
HAVE BOUGHT UNITS OF OUR "BABY DELPHI PLAY SET"

THIS WEEK, IN STORES,
A DOLL TO STIMULATE
YOUNG ADULT FIXATION:
"TEEN DELPHI"
WHO CAN SIMULATE MONTHLY MENSTRUATION.
(LATER, OVER COFFEE, A SMALL DEMONSTRATION.)

(Music vamps as HE points to the picture of DELPHI:)

And on a technical note, Delphi has been outfitted with pain/pleasure implants to assure her complete cooperation … little electrodes placed beneath her scalp here, here and here …

AND ASSURING EVEN DEEPER (EVER DEEPER) PENETRATION.
TAKING THESE EXTRAORDINARY 'Q' LEVELS
TO EVEN NEW LEVELS.
WE CAN EVEN BEAM THE SIGNALS OVERSEAS ...
REMINDING OUR DELPHI
IT'S GOOD TO BE DELPHI —
SO LONG AS WHEN SHE'S DELPHI ...
SHE LIVES TO PLEASE.

COMPLETE COOPERATION ...
TOTAL SUBJUGATION ...
HAPPY IN HER STATION ...
AMAZING PENETRATION ....

(Button and Blackout or optional fade-out into:)

[MUSIC CUE #6A: AFTER AMAZING PENETRATION]

Scene 7

(LIGHTS UP on a movie set, DELPHI working with ZANTH and a DIRECTOR; PAUL is watching from a remove.)

DELPHI. "Oh, Danny — you've given so much to me. How can I —" (*SHE blanks; sweetly.*) I'm sorry. Line, please?

DIRECTOR. Cut! "How can I take anything more from you, when you have so little left to give?" There you go, honey, that's the line.

DELPHI. Any notes?

DIRECTOR. Yes. Act better. (*Turns.*) Okay, lock it up. Speed — action.

DELPHI. "How can I take anything more from you, when you — when you —" (*Blanks again: to DIRECTOR.*) I'm sorry — I — I'm feeling a little dizzy—

DIRECTOR. Cut!! (*HE sighs, goes to her.*) Delphi, honey, we're losing the light. You gonna be okay?

DELPHI. (*SHE raises her arm, revealing a blue bracelet around her right wrist.*) I — I've never worn a body-lift before, Mr. Vere. I guess I'm not used to it.

DIRECTOR. It's no big deal, Dee. Simulated weightlessness. Everybody uses them, they're a kick. Absolutely harmless.

DELPHI. But do I have to wear it while I'm trying to remember my lines?

DIRECTOR. You have to wear it *on camera.* So everyone can see. You do understand that, don't you, Dee?

DELPHI. Yes, but … I don't know if it's really *safe.* Look at this funny blue spot it's made on my wrist —

DIRECTOR. (*Patience wearing thin.*) So take it off between takes.

DELPHI. But the people watching can't take it off between —

DIRECTOR. — What are you, a goddamn consumer advocate?

PAUL. You got a problem with that?

DIRECTOR. (*Outranked; a beat; tightly conciliatory.*) All right. We'll pick up tomorrow, bright and early. You'll have time to memorize your lines — and you'll keep the body lift off until we're ready to shoot. And that's entertainment ... Zanth, I'd like a word with you, please? (*HE exits, followed by ZANTH.*)

[MUSIC CUE # 6B: ON THE SET]

PAUL. (*Crosses to DELPHI.*) Interesting negotiation ploy.

DELPHI. Negotiation ploy?

PAUL. The health of the consumer. I like it even better than the memory lapse bit.

DELPHI. What do you mean?

PAUL. Hey, boss' son, remember? I've seen the old man held hostage by the best.

DELPHI. (*Holds out her wrist.*) Look for yourself. See? It isn't right.

PAUL. Boy, you are really taking this Midwest girl number to the hilt, aren't you?

DELPHI. But somebody has to *do* something about this. If I could just tell your father, *he'd* understand —

PAUL. Let me tell you what my father understands. Pushing products. He doesn't care about little blue spots. His conscience ends at point of purchase.

DELPHI. You don't like your father much, do you?

PAUL. (*A beat.*) I admire him. He believes in what he does and he doesn't care what people think about him.

DELPHI. And you do?

PAUL. ... I guess I care what he thinks.

DELPHI. (*Softly.*) It hurts, caring about what people think of you.

PAUL. ... I never thought you might know about that...

DELPHI. You could always quit. Do something else.

PAUL. Like what? I'm not a kid anymore, I can't reinvent myself. Everything I've been trained to do feeds into the same system. I mean, look around you: this entire film exists so that you can wear that stupid bracelet.

DELPHI. (*Utterly sincere.*) So you see why we have to do something about it!

PAUL. (*Looks at her. A beat. "I give up."*) All right. Okay. I'll talk to my father.

([MUSIC CUE # 6C: THE DATE OF NO RETURN] SHE smiles her thanks as HE turns to go; MUSIC UNDER as HE has second thoughts, stops.)

PAUL. Would you like to have dinner with me tonight? I don't mean as your assistant, I mean ... you know.

DELPHI. You want to have ... dinner ... with *me*?

PAUL. You eat, I know it, I've seen you.

DELPHI. (*A beat. Then, with a shy playfulness:*) Interesting negotiation ploy.

PAUL. (*Laughs, extending his hand.*) Come on.

[MUSIC CUE # 6D: GTX CONTROL PIT]

(THEY exit and LIGHTS COME UP ON ...)

Scene 8

(The lab at GTX Control. ISHAM enters with JOE.)

JOE. We've, uh, had Delphi under surveillance since the reports of trouble on the set, sir and — well, we seem to have gotten footage of her first date with a young man. She's had several in the last few days but the first one rather sets a tone that I thought —

ISHAM. Hopkins, the poor creature deserves a little fun —

JOE. It's who she's having fun *with,* sir …

(HE adjusts controls; LIGHTS come up on PAUL and DELPHI, downstage, walking along a quiet street at night. When ISHAM sees PAUL, HE stiffens.)

DELPHI. Dinner was so wonderful. So … elegant. The wine, the music. And when we walked in, everyone stopped and looked at me, did you see? (*PAUL nods, smiles, enjoying her.*) I've looked in the windows of sophisticated restaurants all my life, but to be on the inside always —

PAUL. I knew it. You're not from the Midwest. Where does the daughter of humble farmers get access to the windows of five-star eateries? Come on, where're you from — really?

DELPHI. (*Suddenly realizing.*) I thought you knew. When you asked me out … I thought you *knew.*

PAUL. No, but now I'm intrigued. So what were you before you became Delphi? (*Kiddingly.*) An insurance adjuster? A substitute cybernetics teacher? Maybe a —

(A BAG LADY has entered and nears them.)

BAG LADY. Please, I'm hungry. Could you spare some change?

DELPHI. (*DELPHI's entire demeanor changes.*) Paul, do you have any money?

PAUL. Oh, come on, you never know what they're going to use it —

DELPHI. (*Full-throttle desperation.*) *Paul, give her some money!*

PAUL. All right, all right. (*HE produces a bill.*) Here.

DELPHI. That's not enough!

PAUL. (*Looks at her, produces a few more.*) Will this do?

BAG LADY God bless you! God bless you both!

(The BAG LADY exits. DELPHI walks a few paces away from PAUL, clearly shaken.)

DELPHI. (*Quietly.*) Thank you.

[MUSIC CUE #7: EYES THAT NEVER LIE]

PAUL. (*Appraises her.*) I don't need to know where you're from anymore. I think I've finally got you figured out.

ISHAM. Jesus Christ.

PAUL.

I KNOW WHAT YOU ARE BEHIND THE MAKE-UP,
THE JEWL'RY,
PUBLICITY ...
YOU MAY SEE A STARLET WHEN YOU WAKE UP...
BUT I SEE
THE UNCORRUPT SIMPLICITY OF

EYES THAT NEVER LIE ...
WINDOWS TO A SOUL ...
INNOCENT AND GUILELESS
AND AS CLEAN AS COUNTRY AIR,
A REFLECTION OF THE WHOLE.
CAPABLE OF BEING MISLED, SURELY;
BUT I AS SURELY KNOW WHY:
GOODNESS PURE AS YOURS
SEES GOODNESS EV'RYWHERE
THROUGH EYES THAT NEVER LIE.

DELPHI. Are you saying … you know who I am … and it doesn't matter?

PAUL No. I'm saying I *don't* know who you are. And it doesn't matter.

EYES THAT NEVER LIE!
PATHWAYS TO THE HEART!
EVIDENCE HOW VIBRANT AND ALIVE THE TRUTH CAN BE
LIKE A TIMELESS WORK OF ART!
EVEN AS I TAKE YOU IN MY ARMS, DARLING,
A BETTER PERSON AM I:
VIRTUOUS, NOT PIOUS;
BRAVE, NOT MERELY RASH.
LET THE WORLD DEFY US
WITH SUPERFICIAL FLASH!
EASY WORLD TO CONQUER,
CONQUER WITH THE PASSION
OF EYES THAT NEVER LIE!
EYES THAT NEVER LIE!

[MUSIC CUE #7A: EYES PLAYOFF]

(THEY kiss and exit — as:)

ISHAM. Hm. I seem to have done my job too well, Hopkins. Tell her to break it off. Immediately.

JOE. What if she won't?

ISHAM. Then remind her of what it would be like being P. Burke again. All day. Every day. Remind her of *that,* Hopkins.

(ISHAM exits. JOE unhappily leaves his console and crosses to P. BURKE's cyber-cabinet. HE touches the control pad and the chamber revolves, revealing P.BURKE. Her eyes open. SHE's on cloud nine.)

P. BURKE. Oh, God, Joe … he's so wonderful … he makes *me* feel so wonderful … *(As JOE helps her out of the chamber.)* Do I really have to come back? To this?

JOE. You've got to exercise this body or the muscles will atrophy. [MUSIC CUE #8: NO ONE CAN DO]

(*Then.*) Tell you what, Phil. We'll take it real easy tonight.

JOE.

TAKE ONE STEP ...
(YOU REMEMBER —)
THEN ONE MORE.
(— WHAT TO DO)
LEAN ON ME IF YOU NEED TO;
LEFT ... RIGHT ... LEFT ...

INHALE AND ...
(DON'T FORGET NOW:)
... EXHALE.
(YOU'RE THINKING FOR TWO)
WORKING OUT'S GUARANTEED TO
KEEP THOSE BRAIN CELLS OXYGENATED,
KEEP THOSE THOUGHTS DELICIOUSLY DEFT.

P. BURKE. I'm so ... clumsy.

JOE. Don't say that!

NO ONE CAN DO WHAT YOU CAN DO, KIDDO.
NO ONE CAN BE THE WHO YOU CAN BE,
MANY HAVE TRIED, BUT FEW CAN DO, KIDDO,
HALF OF THE WHOLE THAT YOU DO FOR ME.
UP I BOLT EACH MORNING LIKE A PISTOL SHOT;
YOU'RE THE JOLT THE STRONGEST COFFEE CRYSTAL'S NOT.
ONCE I WAS JUST A GENERAL JOE,
LIKE SILVER WITHOUT THE STERL.
CUZ NOBODY DID WHAT YOU CAN DO, KID,
AND THAT IS TO BE MY GIRL.

P. BURKE. (*As JOE exercises her.*)

I'LL BE YOUR GIRL ...

JOE.

(ARM ...)

P. BURKE.

THEN I'LL BE HIS GIRL ...

JOE.
(UP ...)
P. BURKE.
AND HOLD HIM FAST.
JOE.
(DOWN)
WE'LL HAVE TO TALK ABOUT THAT.
P. BURKE. (*Oblivious.*)
NO ONE'S LOVED ME ...
JOE.
(ARM ...)
P. BURKE.
OR LET ME LOVE THEM ...
JOE.
(UP ...)
P. BURKE.
BUT NOW, AT LAST —
JOE.
(DOWN.)
LET'S YOU AND ME HAVE A CHAT.
(Screws up his courage.)
PHIL, YOU'LL HAVE TO DROP PAUL.
P. BURKE.
WHY ... ?
JOE.
HIS FATHER WANTS YOU TO ... PLUS ...
P. BURKE.
WHAT ...
JOE.
PAUL WOULD SOON LEARN ...
AND THEN HE WOULD TURN ON YOU.
HE WOULDN'T UNDERSTAND.
NOT LIKE —
(Unable to hold her gaze, back into exercise mode:)
US. NOW *TWIST*,
LIKE I TAUGHT YOU.
OTHER SIDE —
ATTA GIRL!

P. BURKE.
BUT —

JOE. *(Misinterpreting, glancing.)*
LOOKS GOOD.
BREATHE CORRECTLY.
DEEP ... DEEP ... DEEP.
MAKE A FIST.
SQUEEZE IT TIGHT —
NOW LET YOUR FINGERS UNCURL.
(Her fist remains clenched.)
PHIL — HEY — LOOSEN YOUR FINGERS.
(Her arm is white and rigid.)
FINGERS, PHIL, YOU GOTTA LET GO ...
(HE pries her hand open.)
OKAY, PHIL, LET'S PUT YOU TO SLEEP.

(And as HE puts her to bed:)

NO ONE CAN DO WHAT YOU CAN DO, KIDDO.
I KNOW IT'S TOUGH TO BE SO UNIQUE.
ONE LIKES TO DO WHAT TWO CAN DO, KIDDO;
STILL, THOUGH, YOU KNOW, IT ISN'T ALL BLEAK:
HAVE SOME FAITH THAT EVEN IN A WORLD OF DOUBT,
SOMEONE, SOMEWHERE UNDERSTANDS YOU INSIDE OUT.
ONE DAY, PERHAPS, YOU'LL REALIZE WHO,
ASSUMING YOU HAVEN'T GUESSED.
A WHO WHO'S A-WHIRL WITH WHAT YOU DO, GIRL,
AND THAT IS TO BE ...
THE BEST.

(Button. [MUSIC CUE # 8A: DREAMLAND] LIGHTS DOWN. When P. BURKE gets up off the bed, SHE is in some undefined limbo. The music is agitated. Then DELPHI appears.)

[MUSIC CUE #9: WORTH IT]

DELPHI.
ALL RIGHT!
WE GO TO PAUL AND TELL THE TRUTH!
P. BURKE.
NO, WE CAN'T!
DELPHI.
YES, WE CAN!
IT'S THE HONESTY HE LOVES
(*Of her physical attributes:*)
AND NOT ALL THIS!
P. BURKE.
BUT WE'VE ALREADY LIED TO PAUL!
DELPHI.
BUT IT'S NOT CUT AND DRIED!
IF WE TELL HIM WHERE WE STARTED FROM —
P. BURKE.
— HE'LL LEAVE US!
HE'LL ACCUSE US OF BETRAYAL AND HE'LL LEAVE US!
DELPHI.
GIVE YOURSELF A LITTLE CREDIT, WOULD YOU PLEASE!
HE GOT TO *KNOW* YOU!
NOW HE'LL KNOW A LITTLE MORE AND *UNDERSTAND* YOU.
P. BURKE.
SO, YOU THINK HE REALLY FELL IN LOVE WITH ME?
DELPHI.
YES!
P. BURKE.
AND IF SO, IS HE IN LOVE ENOUGH TO SEE?
CUZ IF HE'S NOT —
WHAT HAVE WE GOT?

(Music changes tone.)

IS IT WORTH IT?
DELPHI.
WHAT?
P. BURKE.
RISKING THE GOOD LIFE?
DELPHI.
OH.
P. BURKE.
ALL THE LIFE THAT WE'VE EVER KNOWN?
ONCE AGAIN TO BE HOMELESS AND ALONE ...
WE COULD LOSE IT ALL ...
DELPHI.
BUT IS IT WORTH IT — ?
P. BURKE.
— WHAT?
DELPHI.
LOSING HIS LOVE?
P. BURKE.
AH, THAT.
DELPHI.
ALL THE LOVE THAT WE'VE EVER HAD?
DIF'RENT KINDS OF ALONE.
P. BURKE.
BOTH BAD.
DELPHI.
BUT IS ONE ... *LESS* BAD?
BOTH.
HE WOULD HOLD ME
IF I TOLD HIM
WHEN THE LIGHTS WERE DIM;
REASSURE ME —
FOR THAT WOULD BE JUST LIKE HIM.
BUT SUPPOSING
HE SHOULD FREEZE
WHEN THE LIGHTS COME ON ...
THOSE ASSURANCES PASS LIKE A BREEZE ...

P. BURKE.
YOU SAY PLEASE.
DELPHI.
AND HE'S GONE.

WHAT'S IT WORTH,
EVEN IF I COULD KEEP HIM,
P. BURKE.
TO STILL KEEP HIM FROM PART OF ME?
BOTH.
LOVE'S A LIE
IF I NEVER TELL HIM —
DELPHI.
STOP AND SEE ME …
P. BURKE.
STOP AND SEE ME …
BOTH.
IS IT WORTH REVEALING WHAT NEVER SHOWS?
(As THEY drift apart.)
FOR WHATEVER IT'S WORTH …
HERE GOES …
HERE GOES.

[MUSIC CUE # 9A: THE PLOT THICKENS]

Scene 9

(The lab at GTX Control. ISHAM enters above as JOE watches DELPHI, pacing, below.)

ISHAM. (*To JOE.*) More tape?

JOE. No, sir, this is live from her dressing room on the set. She called him a little while ago. Surveillance had him just arriving on the lot.

PAUL. (*Enters.*) Delphi? … I got here as soon as I could.

DELPHI. *(A breath; screws up her nerve.)* Paul, I have something to tell you.

[MUSIC CUE # 10: EYES THAT NEVER LIE — Reprise]

PAUL. I've got something to tell you too. You first.
DELPHI. I'm — not what you think I am ...
ISHAM. Does Delphi know about Pain/Pleasure controls?
JOE. Yes, but I told her we would never use them on *her* ...
PAUL. Delphi, nothing you could say would make any difference to me.
DELPHI. Don't be so sure.
ISHAM. Open a channel, Hopkins.
JOE. But she's cooperating, sir.
ISHAM. No, she's telling the truth. *Do* it.
DELPHI. Paul, I wasn't ... like this ... eight months ago —
PAUL.
THE THINGS MY FATHER MAY HAVE DONE TO YOU
MATTER NOT.
DELPHI. Paul, listen to me —
PAUL.
IT SEEMS MY HEART MUST ALWAYS RUN TO YOU
NO MATTER WHAT.
DELPHI. Don't make this harder on both —
PAUL.
THE TIME HAS COME AT LAST
TO GO WHERE MY INSTINCTS CARRY ME.
AND THEY SAY, "MARRY ME" ...
I LOVE YOU.
MARRY ME.
ISHAM. Oh, this is obscene.

DELPHI. (*Softly.*) Thank you. I never thought anyone would ever ask me that, but … I can't.

PAUL. (*Takes her by the arms.*) Delphi, just *quit.* If you will, I will. Loving you, I know it's possible!

DELPHI. Paul, no, you don't understand!

PAUL. I understand better than you think!
ONE CAN GET ADDICTED TO THE GLAMOUR …

ISHAM. Hopkins …

PAUL.
THE MONEY …

ISHAM. Adjust band width …

PAUL.
THE EMPTY FAME …

ISHAM. Pain signal.

JOE. But, sir …

PAUL.
EASILY CONFLICTED BY THE CLAMOR …
BUT HONEY …
IT'S STILL IN YOU TO QUIT THE GAME
FOR EYES CAN NEVER LIE.
YOURS SAY YOU ARE STRONG!
YOURS SAY YOU CAN FLY — YES: *FLY* —
AWAY FROM ALL THE TANGLE
TO MY SIDE WHERE YOU BELONG!

ISHAM. We'll just give her a small warning, Hopkins.

PAUL.
TRUST YOURSELF AS *I* TRUST YOU TO CHOOSE,
DELPHI,
BETWEEN MY FATHER AND ME …

ISHAM. On my mark.

PAUL.
YOU'VE EYES THAT NEVER LIE.
NOW JUST REVERSE THE ANGLE …
AND TELL ME WHAT THEY SEE …

DELPHI. Paul, listen to me! My name is Philadelphia! Philadelphia Burke!

ISHAM. Now!

JOE. Sir, I can't!

DELPHI. This is not who I really am! Eight months ago I was a —

(ISHAM muscles JOE aside, slams a key home, and DELPHI suddenly shrieks in pain. ISHAM smiles with satisfaction as DELPHI grabs her head.)

PAUL. *Delphi!* What the hell *is* it, what's *wrong*?

JOE. Sir, that's *enough,* that's *too much current.*

(JOE pulls ISHAM's hand off the controls and DELPHI's pain ceases. PAUL tries to pry loose DELPHI's fingers.)

PAUL. Delph, let *go,* let me see. (*And now HE sees the electrodes.*) What the hell are *these … ?*

DELPHI. (*Staving away unconsciousness.*) Ask … your father … (*And SHE blacks out.*)

PAUL. (*Of course.*) My father …

[MUSIC CUE #11: ACT I FINALE]

(PAUL picks DELPHI up. LIGHTS isolate PAUL and ISHAM in brief tableau. Continuous action into …)

Scene 10

(PAUL turns upstage, facing ISHAM as LIGHTS come up full on GTX Control. MUSIC UNDER as ZANTH and SHANNARA appear briefly, now omniscient observers.)

ZANTH.
SOMETHING UNKNOWN …

SHANNARA.
OUT OF CONTROL …

JOE. Sir, he's outside our wing of the building now. What should we do? I can have Security take Delphi from him, he'll never have to find out what she really is —

ISHAM. And he'll never rest until he does. It's too late. Let him in.

JOE. But, sir, you said —

ISHAM. Let … my … son … *in!*

ZANTH.
SOMETHING THAT'S GROWN …

SHANNARA.
OUT OF THE SOUL …

(PAUL enters GTX Control, carrying DELPHI, as ZANTH and SHANNARA vanish. [Note: this next sequence moves like a shot. Even though P. BURKE is visible in her cyber-chamber, PAUL is too monolithically concerned with DELPHI to notice … and the staging must not give him time *or* opportunity *to notice.])*

PAUL. You did this. You undo it.

ISHAM. Hopkins. (*HE crosses to DELPHI's cyber-chamber and opens it.*)

PAUL. *Help* her, dammit!

JOE. (*Takes DELPHI from PAUL; as HE carries her to the cyber-cabinet:)* Severe trauma to the Host. If we're not careful it could feed back into the Operator. (*As JOE attends to DELPHI with a hypo …*)

PAUL. Operator? What the hell is he talking about?

ISHAM. You'll find out soon enough.

DELPHI. (*Revives, weakly.*) Paul … ?

PAUL. (*Rushes to her side.*) Delphi, honey, are you all right?

DELPHI. Paul … has he told you?

PAUL. Told me what?

DELPHI. (*Looks around.*) I want to show you something I can do.

JOE. No, Phil, not in your condition, not like this. The shock could ki —

ISHAM. Stay out of it, Hopkins! The choice is hers!

(HE backs off. SHE looks at PAUL,sings softly.)

DELPHI.
ONCE UPON A WISH,
I'D'VE WISHED THAT LIFE WERE FAIR …
ONCE UPON A WISH,
I'D'VE WISHED FOR NO MORE FEAR …
ONCE UPON A WISH,
I'D'VE WISHED FOR ONE MORE CHANCE …
NOW I ONLY WISH
TO GO FROM HERE …

(Her eyes close and her body goes limp as, opposite, non-stop, P. BURKE revives, picking up the thread, a ripple of intense pain passing through her.)

P.BURKE.
TO HERE …

(As SHE sings, PAUL turns, slowly begins to realize. And gradually, HE is drawn to her.)

P. BURKE.
ALL THAT I GOT TO DO …
ALL THAT I GOT TO BE …
FINALLY SEEING, THE THING MOST WORTH BEING
IS NOBODY ELSE BUT ME …
JUST TO FIND, AS I ALWAYS KNEW I WOULD …
THAT SOMEDAY, SOMEONE …
THAT SOMEHOW, SOMEONE …
MIGHT STOP … AND SEE ME …

Paul ... I love you ...

PAUL. (*Moves slowly toward P. BURKE ... and:*) I ... I love you too.

P. BURKE. (*Smiles, finally at peace.*)
GOOD.

(SHE is seized by a gentle wave of pain, closes her eyes, stiffens — and life leaves her. PAUL touches her throat lightly, feeling for a pulse — but there is nothing.)

ISHAM. Hopkins, we'll be needing a replacement for Ms. Burke. Get on that, will you? (*JOE just stares at ISHAM.*) Hopkins ... ? (*Defeated, JOE exits to obey. And ISHAM turns his attentions on PAUL.*) "I love you, too ..." It was noble of you to lie to her in the end. I can't say I'd've done the same.

PAUL. I wasn't lying, you murdering son of a bitch.

ISHAM. I wasn't responsible for her death. She did everything voluntarily. Even that.

PAUL. And you let her. Knowing that I was in love with her.

ISHAM. (*Indicating DELPHI.*) No, you were in love with *her*. The beautiful blonde that I created! You're the perfect consumer, Paul. You fell for the package.

PAUL. I would have loved her no matter what she looked like!

ISHAM. A bag lady? *You wouldn't even give a street woman some change until the beautiful blonde begged you to do it!*

PAUL. (*Closes on his father.*) How did you — (*Stops at ISHAM's expression. Hushed rage, barely contained.*) I'm gonna take you down. I'm gonna expose you and your whole Empire. (*HE starts to exit and*—)

ISHAM. (*Quickly.*) Paul, wait a minute ... Why not run it with me instead? I think you *can,* now. I think you're *ready.*

PAUL. (*Appraises his father. Then*:) You know what? I don't care what you think. I'm done here. (*Starts to exit, turns*.) And so are you.

ISHAM. (*Stung, but holding it in check.*) Backbone after all. Makes a father proud.

(LIGHTS DOWN.)

EPILOGUE

[MUSIC CUE #11A: ENDGAME]

(A drum roll. LIGHTS change to indicate a jump in time, and over the sound system:)

ANNOUNCER. Ladies and gentlemen, put your hearts and hands together for the esteemed founder and Chairman of the Board of GTX … Mr. Theodore S. Isham!

ISHAM. (*Addresses the audience.*) Ladies and gentlemen. Members of the press. It's been six months since the sudden illness which nearly cost our beloved Delphi her life. But, happily, our latest and brightest star has made a complete recovery … in fact, you might say she's — a new woman. It's with great pride that we welcome her back to the GTX family! (*A quick beat; the old confidence now subtly cracked*:) As for the completely unwarranted and punitive Grand Jury Investigations of GTX currently underway, let me just say this: I am confident that GTX will be vindicated, and will continue to provide you, our public, with the quality product you so richly deserve.

(HE exits as LIGHTS COME UP on FANS in the street, flanking DELPHI. A different, more calculated DELPHI, lacking the old innocence.)

SECOND FAN. Delphi, Delphi! We're so glad you're all right!

DELPHI. It's so good to be back. All those vidcards and E-mail messages … they helped me get well. I love you all.

THIRD FAN. I love you, too. Can we have your autograph?

DELPHI. Oh, of course. It's the least I can do.

(As SHE signs — PAUL appears on the street. HE takes a step or two closer, as DELPHI finishes signing. SHE looks up to see him staring at her.)

DELPHI. (*After a beat.*) I bet you'd like an autograph too. Well, come on, don't be shy.

PAUL. (*Looking at her wrist.*) You wear a body-lift now?

DELPHI. (*Laughs, displaying it.*) Doesn't everyone? It's a Mercatti. Top of the line. (*PAUL keeps staring at her. SHE drops the pose, briefly, struck by the intensity of his gaze.*) I'm sorry, have we met before?

PAUL. No. I was just wondering — (*Pointedly.*) Don't the little blue spots get to you?

(SHE is finally, genuinely unnerved. Affecting a regal poise:)

DELPHI. Excuse me.

(SHE breezes past him, returning to her adoring fans as HE crosses to the other side of the stage. ZANTH and SHANNARA appear, omniscient observers once again.)

ZANTH and SHANNARA.
TELL US O STARS ABOVE:
IS IT A BRAVE, NEW LOVE?
WILL IT BE BURNING OUT
OR BURNING BRIGHT …

(PAUL and DELPHI, over this, cross to opposite sides of the stage. SHE finishes giving autographs and the FANS leave.)

ZANTH and SHANNARA.
WHEN IT'S A WEIRD ROMANCE …

(Something stops PAUL from exiting …)

REALLY A WEIRD ROMANCE …

(An odd, unsettled look crosses DELPHI's face …)

THOROUGHLY WEIRD ROMA-A-*ANCE* …

(And at precisely the same moment, PAUL and DELPHI turn their heads, and look at each other across the expanse.)

TONIGHT?!!

BLACKOUT

[MUSIC CUE #11B: ACT I PLAYOFF]

ACT II

Scene 1

[MUSIC CUE #12: OPENING ACT II]

(In the darkness, over sustained chords, a disembodied FEMALE VOICE sings:)

VOICE.
SOMETHING THAT'S GROWN
OUT OF THE SOUL
THIS IS A WEIRD ROMANCE ...

(Hot jazz music from the Forties. Then LIGHTS COME UP on a figure — a tuxedoed band singer, JOHNNY BEAUMONT, bathed in weird, prismatic light, otherworldly and beautiful.)

JOHNNY BEAUMONT.
YOU SAY YOU KNOW LOVE AND ROMANCE
WELL MAYBE YOU THINK YOU DO;
BUT, BABY, JUST GIVE ME HALF A CHANCE
I CAN SHOW YOU A THING OR TWO
I CAN SHOW YOU A THING
(RING-A-DING, RING-A-DING)
OR —

[MUSIC CUE #13: MY ORDERLY WORLD]

(HE FREEZES, as LIGHTS COME UP on the set, and:)

DANIEL. (*With awe and wonder.*) Perfect. Just perfect. There's not a holographic imaging system anywhere in existence like this. (*Looks over at KEVIN.*) You want to gloat or something, it's okay.

(We're in a computer lab, filled with state-of-the-art equipment, including a control console and hologram chamber. Two men in labcoats, KEVIN and DANIEL, make adjustments as they watch BEAUMONT.)

KEVIN. (*Abstracted; moody.*) Resolution's off on that one. Make a note to work on it. (*And.*) Bring in the next image.

DANIEL. (*A short sigh.*) Sure. (*As another figure, a BOXER, appears in the holo chamber.*)

YOU'RE NOT HAPPY IN YOUR WORK, DOC.
YOU OUGHT TO SMILE MORE.
I MEAN IT'S NOT LIKE WHAT YOU'VE DONE HERE
HAS EVER BEEN DONE BEFORE.

KEVIN. Focus, dammit.

DANIEL. Focus.

LIGHTEN UP, DOC.
TAKE A TIP FROM UNCLE DAN.
THE BOYS FROM CORPORATE SEE THIS,
THEY'RE GONNA CANONIZE YOU.

KEVIN. Rotation.

DANIEL. Rotation. (*Makes an adjustment; the FIGURES pivot, rotate.*)

SO ENJOY, DOC.
THIS PROJECT AIN'T MEANT TO FOLD.

KEVIN. Next?

DANIEL.

TODAY'S THE DAY I BECOME A FOOTNOTE
AND YOU THE NEXT *OMNI* CENTERFOLD.
YOU'RE BEYOND YOUR RIVALS BY LIGHT YEARS …
SO COME ON, DAN'S BUYIN' THE LITE BEERS.
WHATTAYA SAY?
ME AND YOU?

DOCTOR DRAYTON?

KEVIN. Mm? I'm sorry, Dan, I wasn't listening.

DANIEL. (*A beat.*)

YEAH.

BOTH.

WHAT ELSE IS NEW?

(LIGHTS isolate KEVIN and HE sings his thoughts:)

KEVIN.

MADE OF LIGHT
I PROJECT,
MY ORDERLY WORLD.
FULL OF SOUNDS
I SELECT,
MY ORDERLY WORLD.
FROM A GRAIN ON A BEACH
AND THE ATOMS WITHIN
TO THE STARS OUT OF REACH
THAT FOR ME ALONE SPIN,
EV'RY PART
OF THE WHOLE,
IMAGINED OR REAL:
MINE TO CHART,
TO CONTROL,
TO CHOOSE TO REVEAL.
WANT 'EM SCANNED?
WATCH THE AIR.
I COMMAND —

(HE tabs a key; a BRIDE appears in the chamber, perpetually "throwing" her wedding bouquet.)

AND IT'S THERE.
AS I PLANNED
IN MY CAREFUL, ORDERLY WORLD.

AND I KNEW, THROUGH THE BIRTH

OF MY BRILLIANT APPLIANCE
THAT IT COULD CHANGE THE EARTH;
THAT IT WOULD ALTER SCIENCE;
THAT I'D BE, IF I WANTED TO,
THE FAIR-HAIRED KID …
IF I GOT IT RIGHT.
AND — LOOK AROUND —
I DID!

(HE flips a switch and now ALL THREE FIGURES box, dance, move simultaneously … then just as suddenly HE freezes them. During the following, one by one, THEY disappear.)

SO IT'S DONE.
MEANING WHAT?
IT'S COME TO A CLOSE.
IS IT FUN?
IT IS NOT.
IT'S GOOD I SUPPOSE.
IT'S A GOAL,
IT'S A DREAM,
IT'S A TORCH TO PASS ON;
YET I FEEL NO EXTREME:
I'M AN AUTOMATION
I FINISH, I'M GONE
AND NOT A LIGHT I PROJECT
CAN ALTER MY VIEW,
NOR A SOUND I SELECT
SAY ANYTHING NEW.
IF YOU FEEL NO THRILL OF TRIUMPH,
DOES IT MEAN YOU DIDN'T WIN?
WHERE'S THE JOY?
WHERE'S THE PRIDE?
WHERE'S THE TOY SURPRISE INSIDE?
WHY AM I SO OUT OF PLACE IN
MY ORDERLY

(The last FIGURE disappears.)

WORLD … ?

(A beat … and the phone rings. KEVIN snaps out of his reverie, picks it up. LIGHTS COME UP on the Drayton home; CAROL DRAYTON cradles the phone against her shoulder as SHE slips on a bracelet, a necklace, etc.)

KEVIN. Drayton …

CAROL. Kev? Hi. What time did you make the reservations for?

KEVIN. (*KEVIN's entire body language changes: becomes tauter, tenser.*) I forgot.

(Behind CAROL, her partner REBECCA appears, trying not to eavesdrop.)

CAROL. An hour ago you told me you'd made them—

KEVIN. I know. I was going to call, but I got wrapped up in work, and —

(REBECCA catches CAROL's eye, holds up a sheaf of papers.)

CAROL. Hold on a second, Kev, Becky's just leaving. (*Cupping mouthpiece.*) So you're handling paste-up on the Greybriar ad?

REBECCA. And you're doing the roughs for the Matheson layout?

CAROL. Right.

REBECCA. That Kevin?

CAROL. Uh huh.

REBECCA. Tell him he doesn't deserve you. Hi, Kev.

KEVIN. Hi, Beck.

REBECCA. *(To CAROL.)* 'Night, hon.

CAROL. 'Bye, Beck. (*As REBECCA leaves; into phone.*) Sorry. Kev, why didn't you just tell me you hadn't made them, I could've done it —

(DANIEL, overhearing this, tries to look busy at a keyboard. Both HE and KEVIN have their backs to the hologram display.)

KEVIN. Look, why is this such a big deal? Just make the reservation at Jacob Wirth's and I'll meet you there at seven, okay?

(And now something strange is happening in the holo chamber — its doors have quietly opened to reveal an image, bathed in the same prismatic light, of what appears to be … a human fetus, rocking gently, as though in some invisible womb …)

CAROL. (*Gently.*) Kev, I know you don't want to talk about this tonight, but —

KEVIN. (*Snappish; pre-empting.*) Carol, I've got to go. I'll see you later, okay?

(And HE hangs up. LIGHTS DOWN on CAROL and the Drayton home. [MUSIC CUE #13A: FETUS ENVY] KEVIN sighs, turns … and sees what's inside the holo display.)

KEVIN. What the hell is this?

(DANIEL turns. Startled. Long beat.)

KEVIN. Did you just call this up?

DANIEL. No. It's not even part of any of our programs. (*Fascinated, HE moves closer to inspect it.*)

KEVIN. What is it?

DANIEL. Looks like a …

KEVIN. What?

DANIEL. A fetus. A human fetus …

(And indeed, we even hear, through the lab's speaker systems, the sound of an embryonic heartbeat. KEVIN looks unnerved.)

KEVIN. (*Long beat, then.*) If this is a joke, now would be a good time to let me in on it.

DANIEL. If it's a joke, it ain't mine. (*Re: fetus.*) Actually, it's pretty cool. Pretty far along … eight, maybe nine months …

KEVIN. (*Flat.*) Dump it.

DANIEL. (*Surprised.*) Don't you want to find out where it's coming from?

KEVIN. Someone in the Comp Sci lab's having some fun at our expense.

DANIEL. Jacobi.

KEVIN. That bastard, this is just the kind of warped practical joke he'd pull.

DANIEL. Look at the detail, someone put a lot of work into this —

KEVIN. (*Turns away, continues to get ready to leave.*) Just dump it and let's get on with our lives.

(DANIEL is disappointed, but HE goes to the control console and works the keyboard. Turns. It's still there. Works the keys again. And again. And again. The fetus stubbornly remains. And the heartbeat gets louder. DANIEL straightens.)

DANIEL. Damn …

KEVIN. What?

DANIEL. I can't dump it. (*Off KEVIN's reaction.*) I got all the error-correcting codes running, I did all the debug routines this morning —

KEVIN. Then abort the program. Reset the system.

(DANIEL returns to the keyboard ... but to no effect. Impatiently, KEVIN shoulders DANIEL aside.)

KEVIN. Here, let me look —

(HE starts working the console. DANIEL stares, with mounting fascination, at the fetus.)

KEVIN. Come *on,* dammit —

(HE punches in a code — then another — and another ... and then, at last, the holo display shuts down, the chamber doors close. DANIEL's as disappointed as KEVIN is relieved.)

KEVIN. *Finally.* (*Straightens; sighs.*) Stubborn little bugger, wasn't it?

DANIEL. Yeah, but where the hell did it come from?

KEVIN. Something that sophisticated has to leave tracks. If it *was* Jacobi, I'm going to nail him to the wall. Tomorrow. Tonight, I'm late for dinner.

(HE changes into a sports jacket. DANIEL continues to stare at the hologram chamber.)

DANIEL. You know, Doc, it almost seemed ... *alive...*

KEVIN. Probably was. Video of a real fetus, computer-enhanced. C'mon, Dan, don't get weird on me. G'night.

[MUSIC CUE #13B: BABY COMES TO LIFE]

(DANIEL nods, uncertain. KEVIN exits; DANIEL flips off the lights, though not without a backward glance. HE exits. A beat, and ...

The holo display activates by itself, light spilling out from behind the closed chamber doors — and we hear the sound of a BABY crying ... a squalling, squirming, newborn infant ...)

Scene 2

(KEVIN enters. HE sits, starts sifting through paperwork. CAROL appears in a sexy negligee.)

CAROL. (*Playfully.*) Dr. Drayton? (*Mimicking a paging system.)* Dr. Drayton, you're wanted in insemination.

(SHE leans in to kiss him, but HE gets up, brushes her aside.)

KEVIN. Carol, c'mon, I gotta read this —

CAROL. (*A beat; sighs.*) Kev, I'm trying to understand. You knew when we married that I wanted children. I thought you wanted them, too.

KEVIN. I *do*. I just don't ... feel ready. There's still too much to do at the lab, and —

CAROL. (*Suddenly angry.*) To *hell* with the lab. I barely even see you anymore, and when I do, all you can talk about is the damn *lab*.

KEVIN. It's three years of my life, Carol! I can't just throw that away, can I?

CAROL. (*A beat; trying to understand.*) Kev, what is it? What's bothering you?

KEVIN. (*This sounds unconvincing, even to him.*) I've just been under a lot of pressure to get the project done. That's all.

CAROL. (*Not an accusation.*) You've been under job pressure before. (*Afraid to voice her next thought.*) Is it that you don't want to have children? Or is it ... that you don't want to have children with *me*?

KEVIN. That's not it. It's — (*HE pauses, unable to put whatever he's feeling into words; feeling suddenly crowded, suddenly threatened. Abruptly, HE grabs up a pillow and a blanket.*) I'm sorry. I can't handle this right now. I've got to be alone for a while. Okay?

CAROL. (*Tight; suppressing her anger.*) Sure. Fine. Whatever you want.

[MUSIC CUE #14: ORDERLY WORLD—Reprise]

(KEVIN moves off, as CAROL sings:)

CAROL.
WHY AM I SO OUT OF PLACE IN
HIS ORDERLY WORLD ...?

(LIGHTS FADE.)

Scene 3

(The lab is dark. Fading up, the sound of a CHILD singing to itself. The hologram chamber MOVES FORWARD on its tracks, the doors opening to reveal — a five-year-old GIRL.
KEVIN enters ... and stops short.)

KEVIN. What the —

(The GIRL — NOLA — looks up, eyes bright and innocent.)

NOLA. Hi!

KEVIN. (*Stares, flabbergasted, for several beats ... then, suddenly, laughs.*) Very good. *Very* clever, Jacobi. You access the computer ... feed in a prerecorded tape that trips when the door opens ... even calculate the angle to have her look at me ... this is good —

NOLA. (*Puzzled.*) *What's* good?

KEVIN. (*Goes white.*) Jesus Christ! You can't do that, you can't answer me —

(DANIEL enters, at first oblivious.)

KEVIN. Daniel —

DANIEL. (*Sees NOLA; a take.*) What the hell is that? (*As HE moves closer.*) Oh, this is great — (*HE moves to the holo field, puts out a hand as if to frame the image in his eye.*) This is fantastic —

NOLA. (*Repeats the gesture, taking it for a wave.*) Hi!

(DANIEL looks to KEVIN. No help there.)

DANIEL. Uh ... hi. (*To KEVIN.*) Tell me it's an artificial intelligence program.

KEVIN. No "program" can act that spontaneously.

DANIEL. I know. Tell me anyway.

(HE looks at NOLA. SHE waves. HE waves back, smiling wanly.)

KEVIN. Okay. Someone could be ... tapped into the computer. They could be manipulating the image by remote control, talking "through" her like a ventriloquist.

DANIEL. Except for one thing. There are no video inputs for the computer. How the hell does she *see* us?

(KEVIN has no answer. DANIEL moves to NOLA, KEVIN following.)

DANIEL. Uh ... hi again.

NOLA. Hi.

DANIEL. Ah … my name's Daniel. And this is Dr. Drayton … What's your name?

NOLA. Nola.

KEVIN. Nola. You … have a last name, honey?

(NOLA'S face screws up in concentration as SHE tries to get the big word right.)

NOLA. Nola … Granville.

KEVIN. "Nola Granville."

DANIEL. Pretty name. Where do you live, Nola?

NOLA. (*Thinks; then.*) Weschesser.

DANIEL. You mean … Westchester? In New York?

NOLA. (*Nodding.*) In a big green house 'cross the way from the sprained lake.

KEVIN. (*To DANIEL.*) The what?

DANIEL. Grassy Sprain Lake?

(NOLA nods. DANIEL squats down.)

DANIEL. Nola? Honey? What are you … doing in here?

NOLA. (*Unfazed.)* Isn't this where I'm *supposed* to be?

DANIEL. (*Looks at KEVIN.*) You can take this one.

KEVIN. (*Takes DANIEL aside.*) This has got to be some kind of elaborate practical joke. Check out that house. Find out who's living there. Maybe we can get a clue about who's yanking our chain.

DANIEL. You got it.

(DANIEL exits, leaving KEVIN alone with NOLA. [MUSIC CUE #14A: DANIEL LEAVES] Warily, KEVIN squats down. Raises his hand. Moves it back and forth. Watches her track it. SHE looks excited.)

NOLA. Ooh! Is this a game?

(SHE mimics his movements. KEVIN sighs, lowers his hand. Then, an idea:)

KEVIN. Let's play another game. (*After a beat.*) Can you tell what color shirt I'm wearing?
NOLA. White.
DANIEL. And my jacket?
NOLA. Brown.
DANIEL. And my eyes?
NOLA. Blue! Did I win?
KEVIN. (*Miserably.)* I don't know, but I think I lost.

(LIGHTS FADE on all but KEVIN, crossing to his office space, and we're into—)

Scene 4

(Night. LIGHTS UP up on KEVIN's office, where HE pores over printouts and sips coffee. DANIEL enters.)

DANIEL. (*Takes a deep breath.*) There *is* a family living in that house ... and the wife's maiden name *was* Granville. They don't have a daughter named Nola ... but she did recall a great aunt by that name ... kind of a black sheep, she and the family fell out of touch.
KEVIN. Does anyone know where this ... "great-aunt" *is*?
DANIEL. (*Beat; then.*) She died. At least they think so; no one knew the exact date, and county records don't show a death certificate, either. (*And.*) She was born in ... 1917. And that dress our ... guest ... is wearing? It dates from the mid-1920s.

(KEVIN's face goes taut. HE doesn't want to think about the implications of this. A beat.)

DANIEL. Maybe we should ... call somebody in. To study this. Maybe the parapsychology department at Duke—

KEVIN. I've worked on this project for three years! I will not stand by and watch it turn into a New Age goon show, crystal power and dowsing rods!

DANIEL. Yeah, but—

KEVIN. You have any idea what this'd do to our reputations? We might as well say we created cold fusion in a mayonnaise jar!

DANIEL. But if we can find out who she is, why she's here—

KEVIN. I don't want to know! I just want her to go *away*.

DANIEL. (*A beat; troubled.*) All right. This is really starting to piss me off.

[MUSIC CUE #15: NEED TO KNOW]

KEVIN. Welcome to the club.

DANIEL. I'm not talking about Nola. I mean you — your attitude. *(Music begins.)* I passed on a lot of job offers so I could work with you. With Kevin Drayton, the visionary, the pioneer. And now — Dammit, this is the kind of thing I've dreamt about since —
I'M TEN YEARS OLD, I'M AT THE LOCAL DUPLEX:
THE SCIENCE FICTION MATINEE AT TWO.
I DON'T RECALL THE MOVIE,
BUT THE ALIENS WERE GROOVY
AND I WONDERED, HOW'D THEY MAKE THE ACTORS BLUE?
SO —

WHEN I GET HOME, I FILL THE TUB WITH FIZZIES.
THIRTY, FORTY FIZZIES, PURPLE GRAPE.
I SOAK FOR SEVEN HOURS.
I GET THESE FUNNY STREAKS.

THEY WON'T COME OFF IN SHOWERS,
PEOPLE LAUGH AT ME FOR WEEKS.

BUT I KNEW.
THOUGHT I KNEW.
AND AT TEN THAT WAS A MIGHTY HEADY BREW.
ON MY SKIN …
IN MY HAIR …
AND I FELL IN LOVE WITH RESEARCH THEN AND THERE …
AND I THOUGHT,
CHECK IT OUT!:
I'VE LOCKED INTO WHAT MY LIFE IS ALL ABOUT!
AND THUS IT DIDN'T MATTER
WHEN THEY CHUCKLED AT MY HUE.
I WAS TEN,
I WAS BLUE
AND I KNEW.

KEVIN. Is there a point coming anytime soon?

DANIEL. I think you'd better sit down.

IN SENIOR HIGH, I'M TAKIN' HEALTH AND HYGIENE;
BIRTH CONTROL TECHNIQUES ARE WHERE WE'RE AT.
THE TEACHER'S GOIN' ON
HOW BEST AND STRONGEST IS THE CONDOM,
AND I'M WONDERIN': WELL, JUST HOW STRONG IS THAT?
SO —

COMES THE YEARLY SCIENCE COMPETITION …
I SNAP THE SHEET, MY PROJECT IS UNVEILED:
"THE RUBBER PROPHYLACTIC,
HOW IT FUNCTIONS UNDER STRESS"…
THE FACES ON THE FACULTY,
YOU'D THINK I WORE A DRESS.

BUT I KNEW.
HAD IT GRAPHED
FOR THE RUBBER GRIP, THE RESERVOIR, THE SHAFT;
HAD MACHINES
TESTING LENGTH;
LIQUID MERCURY FOR GAUGING TENSILE STRENGTH.
HOW'D I DO?
HARD TO TELL.
SEE, THE *GIRLS* THOUGHT IT WAS INT'RESTING AS HELL ...
THOUGH THE GUYS WERE DOUBLED OVER,
AND THE PRINCIPAL: HOO-HOO!
HE'S OFFENDED,
I'M SUSPENDED,
BUT I KNEW.

(KEVIN tries to interject, but —)

DANIEL.
AND I NEED TO KNOW.
THE UNKNOWN STEPS UP TO DARE ME.
THEN I TELL IT, "YOU DON'T SCARE ME,"
WITH MY HEAD BETWEEN ITS JAWS.
"WHY" — NOW THAT'S A BEAUTIFUL WORD,
THE SECOND BEST THERE IS.
THE VERY BEST THERE IS
IS "BECAUSE."

KEVIN. Meaning?

DANIEL. Meaning this.
I'M ALL GROWN UP, I'M WORKIN' AT THE LAB HERE.
IN SEARCH OF SOMETHING NEW MY DAYS ARE SPENT ...
WHEN THIS HOLOGRAPHIC DEAL
STARTS BEHAVIN' LIKE SHE'S REAL!

SILLY ME, I'M THINKIN': *THIS* IS AN EVENT …
DOC —

IT FRAMES THE SUPERNATURAL IN SCIENCE.
IT CHANGES METAPHYSICS INTO FACT.
IS THERE SOMETHING AFTER DYING,
LIKE AN AFTERLIFE OR GOD?
AND A REASON WHY YOU'RE SIGHING
LIKE YOU FIND MY INT'REST ODD?

I DON'T KNOW.
BUT I WILL.
YOU CAN BET YOUR CHIPS AND DIODES THAT I WILL.
IF IT'S WAR,
THEN IT'S WAR.
CONSEQUENCES NEVER BOTHERED ME BEFORE.
AIN'T THE FAME.
AIN'T THE PERKS.
IT'S THE SIMPLE FINDING OUT HOW SOMETHING WORKS.
I FIGURE, HERE'S A MYSTERY
JUST WAITING TO BE SOLVED.
AND YES, I'M GETTIN' PISSED
'CAUSE YOU DON'T WANNA GET INVOLVED.
GO READ THE JOB DESCRIPTION, DOC,
DISCOVERING THIS SHIT IS WHAT WE DO.
I WANT TO FEEL LIKE I'M TEN
ALL OVER AGAIN,
THAT SWELL TIME
WHEN I WAS BLUE
AND I KNEW …

WHY NOT YOU?

(A long beat; then:)

Look. Do you suppose that somehow … in some way … a human *soul* has been … *reincarnated* … inside that computer?

KEVIN. Dan, I'm not even sure I believe in the human soul, much less in reincarnation!

DANIEL. Why? Why is a soul less believable than any of a dozen sub-atomic particles? We can't prove *they* exist, either.

KEVIN. Yes, but that's *different*. We can posit their existence from the behavior of other, observable phenomena!

(Half-beat. DANIEL goes to the door. Nods in NOLA's direction.)

DANIEL. Yeah? Well that's your phenomena in there, Doc. Go observe.

[MUSIC CUE #15A: OPEN HOLO-CHAMBER]

(A long beat … then KEVIN, challenged, gets up, heads for the door. BLACKOUT on all but him as HE slowly turns upstage, crosses into the lab, and—)

Scene 5

(KEVIN crosses to the hologram display, turns a chair around and sits backwards in it, arms resting on the backrest, and begins talking to NOLA, who is older than the last time we saw her.)

NOLA. Hi, Dr. Drayton.

KEVIN. (*Awkward smile.*) Hi, Nola. You can call me Kevin. Are you … getting bored in there?

NOLA. That's okay. When I do, I just think about stuff.

KEVIN. Like what?

NOLA. (*As HE's intrigued.*) Like just now, I was thinking about the time Daddy took us to the lake for a picnic ... and I was wearing a dress Mama bought for me in New York City? And it was hot, and I just wanted to get my feet wet, so I rolled up my bloomers and went in on tiptoe and — (*Her face clouds over.*)

KEVIN. What's the matter?

NOLA. I ... just remembered what happened next.

KEVIN. What?

NOLA. (*A wounded look.*) Daddy paddled me. Hard.

(A beat as KEVIN takes this in ... then:)

KEVIN. Nola? Do you think you could ... remember some more things for me?

[MUSIC CUE #16: YOU REMEMBER]

NOLA. How come?

KEVIN. Well ... remembering can be very important.

NOLA. Why?

KEVIN. Because if you remember enough, maybe I can begin to underst — (*Another tack.*) That is, maybe I can begin to explain to mys — (*And again; this time with some confidence.*) I know.

DO YOU LIKE CHOCOLATE?

NOLA. Yes!

KEVIN.

HOW CAN YOU TELL? ...
YOU *REMEMBER* ...
THE TASTE AND THE TOUCH
AND THE CHOCLAT-Y SMELL ...
YOU REMEMBER.

YOU REMEMBER YOU HAD IT BEFORE ...
REMEMBER IT MAKING YOU GLAD.
AND LET'S SAY YOU NEVER HAD CHOCOLATE,

YOU'D KNOW THERE'S A MEMORY YET TO BE HAD.

AND IF I KNEW YOU LIKED IT,
I'D PUT SOME ASIDE
FOR THE HAPPINESS THAT IT EXTENDS.
SINCE I'D REMEMBER
THAT *YOU* REMEMBERED,
AND THAT'S HOW FRIENDS LEARN ABOUT FRIENDS.

AND SINCE WE'RE TO BE FRIENDS
AND I'VE SO MUCH TO LEARN …

NOLA.
I'LL REMEMBER!

KEVIN.
VERY GOOD!
I'LL ASK YOU A QUESTION
AND YOU, THEN, IN TURN …

NOLA.
WILL REMEMBER!

KEVIN.
WILL REMEMBER
YOUR STREET—

NOLA.
ON A GREEN, GRASSY HILL.

KEVIN.
YOUR ROOM—

NOLA.
PINK WITH TRIMMING AND TOYS.

KEVIN.
YOUR BROTHERS AND SISTERS —

NOLA.
ONE BROTHER, THAT'S ALL …
AND *HIS* ROOM WAS BLUE, BECAUSE BOYS …
WELL, *FATHER* SAID BLUE WAS FOR BOYS.

KEVIN.
AND YOU PREFERRED BLUE?

NOLA.
I'D'VE TRADED SOME TOYS ...
(Then, suddenly aware ...)
KEVIN, HOW DID YOU KNOW?
KEVIN.
YOUR MEMORIES TOLD ME.
IT JUST TAKES A FEW TO GO FAR.
SO DON'T FORGET
AS YOU KEEP REMEMBERING,
MEMORIES ARE WHO WE ARE.

(KEVIN crosses away from the holo chamber as its doors close; it's a little later now as DANIEL enters.)

KEVIN. You turn up anything more?

DANIEL. School records, voter registration, but still no death certificate. How's it going here?

KEVIN. It's incredible. The older she gets, the more she remembers. As if she's ... existing on two different levels of consciousness, simultaneously.

DANIEL. What do you mean?

KEVIN. One is a remembered past, the other is her real-time presence, here, with us. (*A beat; surrendering.*) *No* one could design a program this sophisticated.

NOLA. *(Off.)* Kevin, I just remembered something else!

KEVIN. (*A bemused shrug.*) I've created a monster.

(LIGHTS RISE on the lab; it is the next morning.)

DANIEL.
SHE'S AGING AT A RATE
ALMOST TOO BIZARRE TO SAY:
FIVE MONTHS EVERY HOUR,
TEN YEARS EV'RY DAY;
AND SHE'S NOT THE ONLY ONE
GOING THROUGH CHANGES
THE DOC IS TRANSFORMING

EACH MINUTE HE SEARCHES FOR MORE …

(The holo chamber's doors open to reveal NOLA, now a pretty seventeen.)

KEVIN.
I WANT TO LEARN MORE.
NOLA.
I WANT TO SHARE MORE.
DANIEL.
TO GET TO THE CORE!

(LIGHTS UP full; DANIEL exits as KEVIN and NOLA sing to each other. Note: underlined words indicate lyrics that overlap or are sung in counterpoint.)

NOLA.
THE FACES AND PLACES
ARE WHIRLING AROUND ME AS —
KEVIN.
YOU REMEMBER —
NOLA.
I REMEMBER —
KEVIN.
YEAR BY YEAR.
NOLA.
I NO SOONER SHARE ONE
WHEN ANOTHER HAS FOUND ME AND —
KEVIN.
YOU REMEMBER —
NOLA.
FOR THE PIECES CONNECT.
KEVIN.
YOU GET CAUSE AND EFFECT …
BOTH.
THINGS YOU DIDN'T EXPECT,
BUT YOU SEE
THAT WHEN YOU REMEMBER,

YOU REMEMBER THE KEY!

NOLA. (*Reflectively.*)
THE KEY TO ME …

KEVIN. (*Approvingly.*)
YOU REMEMBER —

(MUSIC FADES into:)

NOLA. — I remember this one time, Daddy got hold of a book of poetry I was reading … William Butler Yeats? In one poem, Yeats uses the dread word, *copulate,* and Daddy … well, Daddy was neither amused nor enlightened. (*As KEVIN laughs:*) I tried reading him the one that begins, "I will arise and go on now, and go to Innisfree / And a small cabin build there, of clay and wattles made —"

KEVIN. "Nine bean-rows will I have there, a hive for a honey-bee …"

KEVIN and NOLA. (*Together.*) "And live alone in the bee-loud glade."

KEVIN. "And I will have some peace there …"

NOLA. (*Delighted.*) You know Yeats?

KEVIN. I know … *some* Yeats. Did your father like the poem?

NOLA. He didn't let me finish. Took the book away from me, and … (*Quietly.*) — tossed it into the fire. "It's not a girl's place," he'd say, "to think about such things." And whenever I'd ask questions … about politics, or literature … he'd just smile a patronizing little smile, and tell me how beautiful I was. Sometimes I wished I were plain as a doormat … anything so I'd be treated as though I had half a brain! (*Beat, then* —) But you must be bored silly by me and my stories. [MUSIC CUE #17: YOU REMEMBER—Reprise] What about you, Kevin? What's your life like?
(Singing.)
YOUR TURN, I THINK,
FOR A STORY OR TWO …

("You Remember" plays over:)

Tell me everything.

KEVIN. (*Evasive.*) Nothing much to tell, really. About your parents —

NOLA.

KEVIN, COME ON,
LET ME LEARN ABOUT YOU!

("You Remember" plays over:)

Are you married?

KEVIN. (*Holds up ring finger.*) Uh ... yes. Yes, I am.

NOLA. (*Her face falls.*) Oh. (*Quickly.*) What's her name?

KEVIN. Uh ... Carol. So. Tell me about the time you—

NOLA. What's she like? Is she smart? She'd have to be, I bet, for you to marry her.

KEVIN. (*Loosening up a bit.*) Yes ... she's very smart. We met in a night class, five years ago.

(Singing.)

SHE JUST STARTED TALKING, LIKE: BOOM.
AND, LIKE THE CLICHE, HAND IN GLOVE,
FEW MINUTES, WE'RE CHATTING AWAY, LIKE OLD FRIENDS;
AND INSIDE OF A WEEK, I'M IN LOVE.

I'D NEVER HAVE DREAMED
IT WOULD HAPPEN SO QUICKLY—
THAT LOVE COULD SO FIERCELY IGNITE.
BUT NOW I THINK OF IT,
I'M REMEMBERING ...

(HE sees her disappointment.
Spoken.)

Well. Anyway. Yes, she is very bright.

NOLA. (*Genuinely.*) That's ... that's nice. I'm happy for you, Kevin. (*A beat; wistfully.*) She must be a very lucky girl. (*LIGHTS fade. In the darkness we hear:*)

CAROL'S VOICE. Kev, what do you expect me to say?

[MUSIC CUE #18: ANOTHER WOMAN]

Scene 6

(LIGHTS COME UP on the Drayton bedroom. KEVIN is packing a small suitcase on the bed as an angry CAROL looks on.)

CAROL. You spend all night at work, don't even call me — I don't know if you're dead or worse, and now — *(Half-beat.)* What could possibly be so wrong with your project that you have to back and sleep in the *lab*?

KEVIN. If I told you, you'd think I was crazy.

CAROL. We've lived this long with each other's craziness. I think I can stand a little more.

KEVIN. Not *this* crazy …

(LIGHTS isolate CAROL; we're in her head.)

CAROL.
AND DO I BUILD ON THE THINGS I'VE SAID?
THAT WHEN HE DOES BRING HIS JOB TO BED,
IT'S ROUGH, BUT IT DOESN'T THREATEN WHAT WE SHARE.
THAT EV'RY TIME THIS DEBATE REPEATS,
I'M ADDING WEIGHT TO THE SILENT BEATS,
AND I'M CONVINCED THERE'S A WHOLE NEW
TENSION IN THE AIR?

FOR THEN I'D HAVE TO SAY THE REST,
NO MORE THE TRUSTING WIFE …
WHICH IS TO ASK WHAT I'VE LONG SUPPRESSED:

IF THERE IS OR IS NOT ANOTHER WOMAN IN HIS LIFE.

(LIGHTS UP on the entire bedroom again; scene continues.)

CAROL. Kevin — is there ... God, I hate asking this, but — (*A beat.*) Is there someone else?

KEVIN. (*Faces her; deliberately.*) There is only the project.

(LIGHTS isolate KEVIN. His thoughts now:)

KEVIN.
AND DO I SAY THAT I SPEND THE NIGHT
AMONG MIRACULOUS PARTICLES OF LIGHT;
AND THAT I CAN'T RISK A SINGLE MINUTE PASSING BY?
THAT WHAT I LOSE WHEN I'M UNINVOLVED
MAY BE THE MYSTERY FINALLY RESOLVED;
AND THAT THE MYSTERY WOULD HAUNT ME 'TIL I DIE?

FOR THEN I'D HAVE TO SAY THE REST.
AND DARE I TELL MY WIFE
THE LAYERED TRUTH THAT IT WOULD SUGGEST:
THAT THERE IS, AND IS NOT, ANOTHER WOMAN IN MY LIFE?

(Another LIGHT isolates CAROL.)

KEVIN and CAROL.
I FELL IN LOVE AND WAS ASTOUNDED:
IT SEEMED TO ANSWER EV'RY PRAYER.
AND NOW I AM, INSTEAD OF GROUNDED,
SURROUNDED
BY AIR ...

CAROL.
I WANT SO BADLY TO BELIEVE …
KEVIN. (*In canon.*)
I WANT TO SAVE US IF I CAN …
CAROL.
THE GAP IS OH, SO SMALL …
KEVIN. (*An echo.*)
THE DISTANCE IS SO SMALL …
KEVIN and CAROL.
I COULD REACH OUT, BUT WOULD THAT BE RIGHT …
TILL I KNOW, IS ANOTHER WOMAN THERE AT ALL?

(LIGHTS UP on the entire bedroom again.)

CAROL. Kev, I still don't understand —

KEVIN. It's only temporary. Until I can get this … sorted out.

CAROL. (*Beat.*) The project … or us? (*Quietly.*) Are you leaving me, Kevin?

(Confused, torn, KEVIN yells, a brief explosion that actually causes CAROL to flinch.)

KEVIN. I don't *know*! I don't know *anything* any more!

(THEY are both taken by surprise by his vehemence. Awkwardly, HE turns away to finish packing. HE is about to close the suitcase, when —)

CAROL. (*Quiet.*) Kevin. (*HE stops; then, with a small, rueful smile:*) You just packed three pair of mismatched socks.

KEVIN. (*Looks. HE takes some other socks, puts them in.*) Thanks.

CAROL. No problem.

KEVIN.
I'M SORRY.
CAROL.
TAKE CARE.
BOTH.
I MEAN IT …
KEVIN.
I'LL CALL.

(HE closes the suitcase, moves out of the bedroom; as lights fade on CAROL, while holding on KEVIN, we see her, at last, starting to cry. KEVIN, though, is moving … forward.)

[MUSIC CUE #18A: OLDER NOLA]

Scene 7

(LIGHTS UP on the lab. NOLA is now in her early 20s.)

NOLA. Life with my parents was so … regimented. When I would eat, what I would wear, who I could see … They had my life all planned out for me … even down to who I would marry. (*A laugh, as SHE thinks of it.*) There was this one boy … I shouldn't laugh, he was very sweet … we grew up together. My father worked with his father, our families vacationed together … it was just sort of *assumed* we'd marry.

KEVIN. But you didn't love him?

NOLA. How do I say this nicely? He was … about six feet tall, and an inch deep. (*A beat; sobering.*) It wasn't his fault. It was me. I was changing.

[MUSIC CUE # 19: PRESSING ONWARD]

BEING RESTLESS …

FEELING ANXIOUS ...
GROWING BIGGER THAN MY ROOM ...
ASKING QUESTIONS,
TESTING ANSWERS,
OF THE WORLD BEYOND THE WOMB.
AND WHEN I BECAME CONVINCED
THAT THERE WAS MORE THAN JUST ONE PLAN—
PRESSING ONWARD,
MOVING FORWARD, BEGAN.

I told my father under no circumstances would I allow him to tell me who I would marry. He was furious ... but the world didn't end.

(LIGHTS DOWN on the lab, as, downstage, SUSAN WALLACH, nee Granville, 20s, watches as her husband, CHUCK, and DANIEL are going down some stairs to where an old steamer trunk sits, in the Granville home's basement. Through this:)

CHUCK. It's down here. Watch yourself on the stairs —

SUSAN. So you're taking a graduate course in genealogy, Mr. Gaddis?

DANIEL. Yeah. At MIT. I'm doing a time-line for my friend Dave — Dave Granville — sound familiar?

SUSAN. 'Fraid not —

(Through the above, CHUCK has opened the trunk and is burrowing through it.)

DANIEL. I'm pretty sure he's descended from your Aunt Nola, but —

CHUCK. (*Blows dust off a scrapbook; mock joy.*) Honey, we're rich! I found one of the Dead Sea Scrolls.

SUSAN. This is it. My mother showed me this when I was a kid ... I remember thinking how pretty Aunt Nola was, wishing I could meet her — Ah, and here she is.

DANIEL. (*Looks at photo; a bit taken aback.*) That sure looks like — (*Catches himself.*) I mean, that's how … Dave … was told she looked — (*Beat, then.*) Did your mother know anything about her parents?

SUSAN. Her father was a banker. Lost most of his fortune in the stock market crash. It didn't humble him any; he never stopped thinking of himself as *better* than everyone else.

DANIEL. How did Nola adjust?

SUSAN. If anything, she was probably relieved. I gather she'd always felt vaguely guilty about her family's wealth. Very little of it survives today.

CHUCK. Myself, I could stand being a bit more guilty.

SUSAN. Mom said that Nola's gift was for … getting *on* with life. Making the *most* of it.
PRESSING ONWARD … MOVING FORWARD …
ON A NEVER-ENDING TRACK.

CHUCK.
(SUSAN ALSO HAS THE KNACK)

SUSAN.
YOU COULD HATE IT, YOU COULD FIGHT IT;
BUT SHE'D ALWAYS FIGHT YOU BACK.

CHUCK.
(NOW I KNOW JUST WHERE SHE GETS THE KNACK)

SUSAN.
SHE WAS GAME FOR TRYING ANYTHING
BUT STANDING STILL
YES, NOLA HAD THE WILL …

CHUCK.
(YES, AND WHAT A WILL …)

CHUCK and SUSAN.
TO KEEP PRESSING FORWARD …

DANIEL. That was when the family lost contact with her?

SUSAN. 'Thirty-five, 'thirty-six …

DANIEL. What do you think brought it about?

SUSAN. If you knew Nola and her father, the split was inevitable …

(As LIGHTS FADE on the Granville house, they FADE UP again on the lab, where NOLA is now in her late 20s.)

NOLA.
PUSHING OUTWARD … REELING INWARD …
FIGHTING FATHER ALL THE WAY.
WANTING MOTION, WANTING COLLEGE …
FATHER WANTING ME TO STAY.
BUT HE FINALLY RELENTED
AND MY HEART BEGAN TO THROB
ON TO *COLLEGE,* PRESSING *FORWARD* TOWARD—

— Robert. Robert Goldman. He was the most incredible man in so many ways. And politically as far to the left of my father as you can imagine. Robert wanted to get married and move to Boston, where he could set up a law practice for the disadvantaged, and I could get my master's in literature.

KEVIN. What did your parents think of that?

NOLA. Father didn't approve. Of any of it.

KEVIN. Just because of Robert's politics?

NOLA. That too. But also because he was Jewish.

KEVIN. You're kidding.

NOLA. No, he made it quite clear. If I married Robert I'd be … cut off. From him … from Mother … from — (*Her voice catches; very close to tears.*) From everything. The whole family.

KEVIN. Nola. I'm sorry. (*Unthinkingly, HE reaches out to take her hand … then draws back, quickly. But the damage has been done: both now painfully aware of the extent and kind of distance between them. A beat; quietly:*)

NOLA. Kevin? Why am here? Like this, with you? (*Afraid of the next thought:*) Am I ... dead, Kevin? Is that it? Am I a — (*SHE can't say the word.*)

KEVIN. I wish I had an answer for you.

NOLA. I ... I feel like there's ... something I have to *do* ... something I have to *accomplish,* but I can't seem to — *remember* ... (*SHE holds out her hands, palms up, in a gesture of helpless entreaty.*) Help me, Kevin. Help me to remember?

KEVIN. (*Quiet; reassuring.*) I promise.
WE'LL KEEP MOVING FORWARD
TO THE ANSWER ...
TOGETHER ...

(HE reaches into the holo display ... places his hands just below hers ... the two of them joined but separate; entwined, but never touching. As LIGHTS FADE DOWN on the lab —

They FADE UP on a downstage space. DANIEL, notebook in hand, approaches a black man in his 50s, GEORGE LESTER, carrying a briefcase.)

LESTER. Goldman ... sure I remember him. My dad worked on the docks. He got into this tussle with a white guy — the other guy started it, but Dad was the one the company fired. Goldman sued them ... and won. He got my father his job back.

DANIEL. I found Robert's death certificate in county records ... he died in 'Fifty-two ... but nothing on his wife — Nola. Do you know if she's still alive?

LESTER. No, I don't. But I met her once.

DANIEL. (*Trying not to betray his rabid curiosity.*) Really?

LESTER. Yeah, Dad had them over for a kind of victory dinner. I got the feeling they weren't much better off financially than we were ...
BUT THEY WERE FAR TOO HAPPY
TO KNOW THAT THEY WERE POOR

DIDN'T DWELL ON MONEY,
LIKE SOMEHOW THERE'D BE MORE.
LIKE AHEAD OF THEM,
THEY'D FIND THE GOLDEN FLEECE.
THEY WERE COOL WITH THAT.
MORE THAN COOL … AT PEACE.

Sorry I can't be of more help. Have you talked to Goldman's law partner?

DANIEL. I didn't know he had one.

LESTER. I think his name was … Ruskin?

DANIEL. (*Scribbling on his notepad.*) That's great. That helps me out a lot. Thank you. Thank you very much ….

(LIGHTS FADE on DANIEL and LESTER and FADE UP on the lab. NOLA is now in her early 30s.)

NOLA. It was the most amazing summer. Full of so many surprises. So many wonderful surprises.

(As SHE sings, LIGHTS isolate SUSAN, CHUCK and LESTER, now not-quite literal ECHOES of the last few interviews, repeating their key phrases — and others — in backup:)

NOLA.	**ECHOES.**
PRESSING ONWARD …	ONWARD
MOVING UPWARD …	UPWARD
ROBERT'S PRACTICE	
BUILDING	**CHUCK & LESTER.**
STEAM	FORWARD, FURTHER, *OUT* …
	SUSAN.
	BUT SHE'D ALWAYS FIGHT YOU BACK.
FOR THE FIRST TIME,	
	TRYING…
EXTRA MONEY	**CHUCK.**

ALWAYS …

AN EVEN
BIGGER
DREAM

LESTER.
FIND THE GOLDEN
FLEECE …

I'D A PAPER GETTING
PUBLISHED
BY A SMALL LITERARY
PRESS
YES ! YES! YES!
FORGING ONWARD!
(*Alone, in the clear.*)
GETTING PREGNANT!

ECHOES. *(With NOLA.)*
YES! YES! YES!
FORGING ONWARD!

(Held chord.)

KEVIN. Wait a minute. Pregnant? You never mentioned that before.

(Music continues in tempo.)

NOLA. (*With a small laugh.*) I just remembered it.

ECHOES.
PRESSING ONWARD …

NOLA. In an … odd sort of way, Kevin, when I sit here, remembering, it's almost as though … it's all happening for the first time.

(The ECHOES begin to drift offstage, one at a time …)

CHUCK.
MOVING FORWARD …

NOLA. Anyway, the pregnancy was totally unexpected. My doctor told me it'd be difficult for me to conceive a child …

SUSAN.
ON A NEVER-ENDING TRACK …

NOLA. But I guess the child had other ideas!

LESTER.

MORE THAN COOL … AT PEACE.

(The ECHOES gone, NOLA continues and the music continues to swell, gloriously, through —)

NOLA.

SO LITTLE TIME FOR US, ALONE,
WITH BABY ON THE WAY.
SO WE DECIDED IT WAS TIME
TO TAKE A LITTLE HOLIDAY
AT A CABIN IN THE WOODS, NEARBY A STREAM.
JUST LIKE INNISFREE:
REMOTE … AGLEAM …

WALKING ONWARD, BY THE WATER,
NEXT TO ROBERT, HAND IN HAND.
VISTAS OPEN TOWARD A FUTURE
WE COULD FINALLY COMMAND!
WITH A FAMILY, A BOOK BY ME,
OUR LOVE AND OUR CAREERS,
I AND ROBERT FOR THE REST OF OUR YEARS
I AND ROBERT FOR THE REST OF —

(MUSIC DOWN as NOLA suddenly cries out, doubled over in pain, hands clutching her stomach. KEVIN jumps to his feet, watching helplessly as NOLA slowly sinks to her knees with remembered pain.)

KEVIN. Nola! Nola, what's wrong?

NOLA. *Oh, God*! Make it stop, make it *stop*!

(DANIEL enters, still in the jacket we last saw him in, and rushes to KEVIN'S side.)

DANIEL. Doc, what the *hell* — ?

NOLA. Kevin! *Help* me, help —

(And then, all at once, the pain stops ... and her face undergoes a dramatic change: shock; astonishment; sadness. And in that moment, there is a sudden maturity, a wisdom and a knowledge that was not there before.)

KEVIN. Nola, what happened? Are you all right?

NOLA. (*Beat; then.*) I ... I lost it, Kevin. I lost the baby ... (*Softly; with an edge that KEVIN neither hears nor understands.*) I remember now ... (*SHE shuts her eyes. Suddenly, SHE seems much older. A long beat. SHE gets to her feet.*) I ... have to ... be by myself for a while, Kevin. Just a little while ...

(SHE makes a gesture, as if willing the chamber doors to close — and they do. The system shuts down.)

DANIEL. (*Rattled.*) I didn't know she could do that.

KEVIN. Neither did I ...

DANIEL. (*Looks at KEVIN.*) You look like hell, Doc. How much sleep are you getting?

KEVIN. Enough. Couple of hours a night. I can't afford to squander my time with her. (*A beat.*) I've never felt so helpless in my life. And she's as confused by all this as we are.

DANIEL. Is she?

KEVIN. What's that supposed to mean?

DANIEL. We know she's controlling the computer — ordering up the processes needed to simulate her image ...

KEVIN. Autonomic functions. She's no more conscious of doing it than we are of the way our hearts pump blood —

DANIEL. I don't know. She seemed awfully damn conscious of shutting down the system, just now.

KEVIN. I can't explain that. But she's not here for any … ill intent. My God, I've watched her grow *up* … I'd *know* if there were something wrong about her.

DANIEL. Would you? (*After a beat.*) Look … Doc. Maybe this is out of line, but … you're not getting yourself — involved — here, are you?

KEVIN. (*Short laugh.*) "Involved"? With a … a spirit?

DANIEL. Some would say that's what we fall in love with, when we fall in love. A soul. A spirit. (*Beat; pointedly.*) She's aging ten years for every day, Doc. At this rate, she'll be … gone … in three or four days. What then?

(LIGHTS DOWN. [MUSIC CUE # 19A: I CAN SHOW YOU A THING OR TWO — Prologue] A beat … then, in the darkness, we hear MUSIC FADING UP, softly, with the LIGHTS. KEVIN sits brooding, half-listening to JOHNNY BEAUMONT singing, off-stage, "I'll Show You A Thing or Two" … then, suddenly, the holo doors open to reveal NOLA, now 40. KEVIN immediately cuts off the music.)

KEVIN. Nola? Are you all right?

NOLA. (*Nods; softly.*) It was … a long time ago. I was seven months pregnant … and I went into labor. Robert rushed me into the nearest town, but … there was no hospital, just a country doctor. Robert blamed himself for it. If we hadn't gone away, if we'd stayed in town —

KEVIN. But there was no way he could have known.

NOLA. Intent didn't matter to him. Only result — cause and effect. He was a very logical man — maybe too logical. (*Beat; quietly.*) It was a little girl, Kevin. A beautiful little girl … (*Wistfully.*) God, Kevin — I wanted it so badly. The chance to … give someone the kind of love I never had, growing up … (*A beat.*) I … don't feel much like remembering this, just now, Kevin. Do you mind?

KEVIN. No ... I understand ...

NOLA. (*After a beat.*) That music you had on ... was that ... Johnny Beaumont?

KEVIN. That's right. I was running some old film clips through the voice synthesizer.

NOLA. Can I hear some of it?

KEVIN. I can do better than that.

(HE punches a button — BEAUMONT appears in the chamber and SINGS.)

[MUSIC CUE #20: I CAN SHOW YOU A THING OR TWO]

NOLA. He looks so real ...

KEVIN. (*Shrugs.*) Colorized ...

JOHNNY BEAUMONT.

YOU SAY YOU KNOW LOVE AND ROMANCE ...
WELL, MAYBE YOU *THINK* YOU DO;
BUT, BABY, JUST GIVE ME HALF A CHANCE,
I CAN SHOW YOU A THING OR TWO.

YOU SAY YOU HAVE ALL THE ANSWERS,
AND MAYBE *TODAY* THAT'S TRUE.
BUT, BABY, BEFORE TOMORROW STIRS,
I CAN SHOW YOU A THING OR TWO.

NOLA. (*Sways in time with the music, a quiet dreamy smile on her face ...*) Robert and I used to dance to music like this. At the Hotel Vendome. I didn't know how, so at first I just pressed close and let him lead us both around the floor ... Do you dance, Kevin?

KEVIN. (*Shakes head.*) Me? No, I took a course once. The Hindenberg of dance lessons.

NOLA. Oh, c'mon, it's easy, let me show you.

(KEVIN is hesitant, but takes a step toward HER.)

NOLA. Just move like I move ... pretend you're my shadow. Raise your arms as though you're taking my hand in yours ... that's right ...

(Nervously, HE does so. HE starts to sway to the music with her, as:)

JOHNNY BEAUMONT.
I CAN SHOW YOU THE LOVE OF A LIFE
YOU WOULD PRAY FOR!
I CAN SHOW YOU A VIEW OF THE WORLD
YOU COULDN'T PAY FOR!
STAY, FOR —

I KNOW YOU GOT BURNED THE LAST TIME,
BUT THIS'LL BE TIME ANEW.
SO, BABY, IF YOU NEED RESCUE, I'M HERE
TO SHOW YOU A THING OR TWO ...

[MUSIC CUE # 20A: AFTER SHOW YOU]

(Through the above, KEVIN falters but begins to find confidence. HE and NOLA dance, separated not by mere inches but by a dimensional gulf that for an instant they seem capable of breaching ... until KEVIN, suddenly aware of being too *close, pulls back. BEAUMONT turns to "conduct" the orchestra during an instrumental break.)*

NOLA. What's wrong?
KEVIN. Nothing. I just ...
NOLA. Is it Carol?
KEVIN. No, that's not it.
NOLA. (*A beat.*) Have you spoken to her lately?

(HE turns away. Doesn't want this subject broached.)

NOLA. (*Quietly pressing.*) Do you really want to *lose* her, Kevin?

KEVIN. (*Reacts out of proportion to the question asked:*) Don't talk to me about *losing* things! (*Hotly.*) All I know is, the minute you become truly happy in this life — that's when they pull the rug out from under you! *That's* when it's all taken away!

NOLA. (*Nods.*) And if you never *know* happiness ... you'll never have to risk *losing* it.

KEVIN. (*Rattled.*) That's not what I'm saying!

NOLA. Then what *are* you saying?

KEVIN. All I mean is, you never — (*Beat; floundering.*) That is, you don't — (*Longer beat; starting to feel foolish.*) Okay, maybe that's a bad —

(And now it's as though a veil has been partially lifted from him; his anger fades, replaced by a certain — embarrassment.)

KEVIN. (*A sigh, then.*) Teach me some more?

(NOLA smiles. Lifts her arms as if to say ... "Now: shall we continue?" KEVIN grins, quite sheepishly, and turns on the music again. HE joins NOLA again, the two of them dancing as one as BEAUMONT finishes:)

JOHNNY BEAUMONT.
I'M HERE TO SHOW YOU A THING OR TWO ...

Scene 8

(LIGHTS UP on the Drayton home. CAROL, in an artist's smock, is working at some clay, finishing an odd, disjointed abstract piece. REBECCA calls her from offstage.)

REBECCA. Carol?

(CAROL steps back from her work guiltily as REBECCA enters. REBECCA looks at the sculpture, then at CAROL.)

REBECCA. So, this is what you've been doing for the last two days?

CAROL. Obsessively.

REBECCA. I thought you had a deadline on the Matheson layout.

CAROL. It'll get done. If necessary, I'll stay up all night and eat Twinkies. This took priority.

REBECCA. (*Circles it.*) Interesting … What is it?

CAROL. (*Meaningfully.*) What do you *think* it is?

[MUSIC CUE #21: A MAN]

REBECCA. (*Inspecting.*) Well …
PART OF IT IS STRONG,
IN FACT, IT MAY PROTEST TOO MUCH.
PART OF IT IS SENSITIVE,
DISPLAYS A LIGHTER TOUCH.
HERE IT'S EASY, THERE INTENSE.
IT TRIES SO HARD TO PLEASE —
BUT IN THE END, IT MAKES NO SENSE.
THAT IS … UNLESS … OH, GEEZ.

YOU MADE A MAN.

CAROL. Bingo.

REBECCA.
YOU MADE A MAN.

CAROL. Right.

REBECCA.
IT'S SO CONFUSED IT SIMPLY HAS TO BE A MAN.

CAROL. That was my thought.

REBECCA.
I SEE YOU GAVE HIM AN ERECTION.

WHERE'S THE BRAIN?
CAROL.
IT'S IN THIS SECTION.
REBECCA.
HON, I DON'T SEE THE CONNECTION.

(Beat.)

YEAH, THAT'S A MAN …
CAROL.
"ABSTRACTION MAN."
REBECCA.
"ABSTRACTION MAN"?
CAROL.
CUZ IT'S A MYSTERY WHAT KEEPS 'EM IN OUR HEARTS.
REBECCA.
YOU CAN'T LIVE *WITH* 'EM …
CAROL.
YOU CAN'T SELL 'EM FOR THE PARTS.
BOTH.
IT ISN'T ART,
BUT IT'S A STARTLING MAN.
CAROL.
THE GOOD ONES DO COMMUNICATE,
THEY TRY TO MEET YOUR NEEDS.
THEN SOMETHING JAMS THE PORT
THROUGH WHICH THE INFORMATION FEEDS.
THEY WATCH THEMSELVES GO CRAZY
AND THEY KNOW YOU KNOW THEY KNOW.
IT'S ALL SO PIRANDELLO.
REBECCA. *(Thoughtfully.)*
MORE LIKE EDGAR ALLAN POE.

(A beat.)

THEY SEEM SO WARM.
CAROL.

OF WARMTH IMBUED.

REBECCA.

THEN SO REMOTE.

CAROL.

THEY TEND TO BROOD.

REBECCA.

AND WHEN THEY DO,
THEY HAVE THIS FUNKY SET OF RULES …

CAROL.

I KNOW THOSE RULES.
(Reciting.)
DON'T CHEER THEM UP WHEN THEY'RE MOROSE.

REBECCA.

BUT HOVER CLOSE — THOUGH NOT *TOO* CLOSE.

CAROL.

FOR WHEN THEY'RE SUDDENLY VERBOSE …

BOTH.

"PAY ATTENTION, DEAR …"

CAROL.

THEY'RE TALKIN' BOOKS!

REBECCA.

'LECTRONIC TOYS!

CAROL.

EXCITED LOOKS—

REBECCA.

LIKE LITTLE BOYS.

CAROL.

SO CUTE THEY SUCK THE AIR OF PATIENCE FROM YOUR LUNGS.

REBECCA.

AND THEN GO, "WOMEN!," LIKE IT'S *US* WHO SPEAK IN TONGUES.

BOTH.

A GIRL CAN GET,
BUT NEVER "GET" A MAN …

(Music slows.)

CAROL.
SURE, I COULD KILL HIM.
BUT WHO WOULD COOK LASAGNA?
REBECCA.
THAT'S ALL THAT STOPS YOU?
CAROL.
IT'S REALLY GREAT LASAGNA.
REBECCA.
SEX IS NICE.
CAROL.
SO I HEAR.
REBECCA.
'LONG YOU BEEN WITHOUT?
CAROL.
DON'T ASK.
REBECCA.
THAT LONG.
CAROL.
UH-HUH.
REBECCA.
EXPLAINS A LOT.
CAROL.
NO DOUBT.
(Looks again at her sculpture; thoughtfully.)
AND YET, THE MAN:
I MADE "THE MAN";
TO KEEP FROM MAKING ULTIMATUMS TO … THE MAN.
SOME FRESH PERSPECTIVE, SOME DISTRACTION…
LET HIM SORT HIS MESS.
CHRIST, THE HARDEST ACTION
IS DECIDING *NOT* TO PRESS …

I LOVE THE MAN.
REBECCA.
THAT'S HOW THEY GET YOU.

CAROL.
KNOW THE MAN.
REBECCA.
MUCH AS THEY LET YOU.
CAROL.
I SHOULD PACK MY BAGS
AND RENT MYSELF A VAN …
BUT SOMETHING TELLS ME HE'LL RETURN,
JUST LIKE SOME WAYWARD, HOMESICK PUP …
(Suddenly snapping out of it, music snapping back to tempo:)
OR STAY FUCKED UP —
REBECCA.
THEY'RE *ALL* FUCKED UP.
CAROL.
THEY ALL NEED HELP.
REBECCA.
NO, *WE* NEED HELP.
CAROL.
SURE, *WE* NEED HELP
BOTH.
CUZ *THEY'RE* FUCKED UP
JUST LIKE "THE MAN"!

(Button. [MUSIC CUE #21A: AFTER A MAN] Over the applause, both women are laughing, CAROL a little sadly as REBECCA hugs HER and the LIGHTS FADE.)

Scene 10

(LIGHTS UP downstage to reveal the garden of a retirement home. DANIEL walks with JOHN RUSKIN, 80s. HE's frail but alert, absently caressing flowers and buds as HE walks; it is only something in the way HE touches them that tells us HE is blind.)

[MUSIC CUE #22: RUSKIN SCENE]

DANIEL. I appreciate your talking with me, Mister Ruskin. I'm afraid most of Robert and Nola's friends are … ah …

RUSKIN. *(Smiles.)* Most of them are dead?

DANIEL. I'm sorry. I didn't mean to sound … tactless.

RUSKIN. (*Soft laugh.*) I've spent the last fifteen years in darkness, Mr. Gaddis, and I've managed to enjoy life in spite of it. If it's darkness I have ahead of me, I think I can make the best of it.

DANIEL. You knew Robert for how long?

RUSKIN. Twenty years. He and Nola were such lovely people … he with his passion for social justice, Nola and her love of literature, and life …

DANIEL. Did either of them leave behind any kind of — "unfinished business"? Some goal, some dream they never fulfilled?

RUSKIN. Well, in later years, there weren't many dreams left for Robert. Not after Nola died.
(Singing.)
PRESSING ONWARD … AFTER NOLA,
ROBERT RATHER LOST THE WILL.
TURNING INWARD … EVER INWARD …
ALL HIS PASSION GOING STILL.
SUCH A SHAME: SHE WAS SO YOUNG
AND HE WAS, OH, SO MUCH IN LOVE …
ROBERT NEVER QUITE RECOVERED …

DANIEL. (*Startled; interrupts.*) Excuse me, but … exactly when *did* Nola die?

RUSKIN. In … March, I believe. March of … 1944. She was only thirty-two. Such a waste. Such a terrible waste …

DANIEL. *(Stunned.) How* — did she die?

RUSKIN. (*Turns; "looks" straight at him for the first time.*) I thought you knew. She died having a miscarriage.

[MUSIC CUE # 22A: BACK AT THE LAB]

(LIGHTS go down, fast, and then up on:)

Scene 11

(The lab. NOLA, now in her late 60s, early 70s looks affectionately at KEVIN as he dozes on the cot. Then SHE turns, faces a computer console, raises a hand. The console hums; a voice synthesizer clicks on. NOLA'S voice issues from it.)

NOLA'S VOICE. Carol? It's Kev. I'm at the lab ...

(The sentence is repeated — remodulated once, twice, three times, changing from NOLA'S voice into a tinny, robotic voice, then remodulating again until it becomes:)

KEVIN'S VOICE. Carol? It's Kev. I'm at the lab...

(NOLA nods with satisfaction, turns to a nearby phone; a click as the computer "picks up" the phone, then the beeping of a number being dialed. LIGHTS UP on: The Drayton home. The phone rings; CAROL rushes on stage to answer it.)

CAROL. Hello?

KEVIN'S VOICE. Carol? It's Kev. I'm at the lab...

CAROL. Kevin? Are you all right?

KEVIN'S VOICE. I'm fine, honey. And I've missed you.

CAROL. (*Holding back tears.*) I've missed you, too.

KEVIN'S VOICE. I'm ready to come home. But I'm too fried to get behind the wheel. Think you can swing by and give a guy a lift?

CAROL. (*A smile.*) I should make you walk.

KEVIN. You probably should.

CAROL. I'll be right over.

(In the lab, NOLA listens to the last of the conversation.)

KEVIN'S VOICE. Great. Thanks. And … I love you.

(CAROL hangs up; the LIGHTS FADE on her as SHE hurries offstage. NOLA smiles, turns to the still-sleeping KEVIN.)

NOLA. Kevin? Time to wake up.

KEVIN. (*Stirs, looks up blearily.*) Mmphh … sorry … must've dozed off …

(HE sees her, and is startled; it's too soon. Too soon.)

NOLA. (*Calmly.*) It's time for me to go now, Kevin.

KEVIN. (*Gets up; suddenly terrified.*) No …

NOLA. I'm afraid so. I accomplished what I had to … and now it's time to leave.

[MUSIC CUE #23: SOMEONE ELSE IS WAITING]

KEVIN. What? *What* did you accomplish? Why were you here?

NOLA. I was here for you, Kevin.

(An arpeggiated chord — held as KEVIN holds her gaze. And another as:)

KEVIN. (*Startled.*) For … me? (*Half-beat.*) Look … I don't understand any of this, but if what you say is true, then … please. Don't leave.

NOLA. My time is up, Kevin. I'm sorry.

KEVIN. (*Suddenly angry.*) You *can't*! Not *yet.*

NOLA. *I have no choice.*

KEVIN. (*Exploding.*) *No*! Damn it, Nola. I can't lose you *again*!

NOLA. (*Gently.*) Like you lost me before?

KEVIN. Yes! Yes! Like before! Like — (*HE stops, suddenly aware of what he's saying.*)

NOLA. I didn't know from the start. Only after the miscarriage. I wasn't just remembering my pain, Kevin … I was remembering my death. (*Smiles at him now with love and sorrow.*) After that it all became clear …

I LEFT YOU TOO SOON, MY DARLING.
I NEVER MEANT TO GO.

KEVIN. I don't *remember* …

NOLA. You remembered *enough* …

YOU CARRIED ALL YOUR GRIEF
FROM ONE LIFE TO THE NEXT,
AFRAID OF LOSING LOVE ONCE MORE
AND SO …

I HAD TO COME BACK, MY DARLING,
TO DRIVE AWAY THE FEAR …
BY LIVING OUT THE LIFE
WE NEVER GOT TO SHARE
A TOUCH OF EV'RY YEAR,
SO THAT, MY DEAR …

YOU CAN LOVE AGAIN.
OPEN UP: IT'S TIME TO BE FREE …
FREE THE LOVE YOU HELD FOR ME:
SOMEONE ELSE IS WAITING.

BID FAREWELL TO THEN.
ALL I HAVE TO GIVE IS RELEASE,

NOTHING MORE, BUT KNOW THERE'S PEACE:
SOMEONE ELSE IS WAITING.

SOMEONE ELSE IS WAITING.
SOMEONE ELSE IS WANTING.
SOMEONE ELSE IS NEEDING;
SOMEONE YOU NEED TOO;
SOMEONE ELSE DESERVING
AND TO BE EMBRACED.
DON'T LET YOUR LIFE SLIP BY ANEW …
ONE WAS ENOUGH TO WASTE.

GO AND LOVE AGAIN,
NOT, MY LOVE, THE WAY YOU LOVED ME;
JUST AS WELL — BUT DIF'RENTLY:
NEITHER LOVE ABATING …
ONE IN MIND:
YESTERDAY.
ONE IN LIFE,
WITH YOUR WIFE —

KEVIN. (*Softly.*)
AND A BABY …

NOLA.
AND A BABY, IF YOU LIKE.
YES.

KEVIN. (*Spoken; almost a whisper.*) Yes.

NOLA.
SOMEONE ELSE IS WAITING.

(Beat.)

I have to leave now.

KEVIN. No. Wait. Just one minute more. (*HE takes a book from a drawer, hurries back to NOLA. HE looks at her with sorrow and affection.*) Yeats again. Do you remember the one called … "When You Are Old?"

NOLA. (*Nods.*) "When you are old and grey and full of sleep —"

KEVIN. Yes. There's a line here ... (*Reads from book.*)
"Many loved your moments of glad grace,
And loved your beauty with love false or true,
But one man loved the pilgrim soul in you,
And loved the sorrows of your changing face ..."

NOLA. (*A soft, gentle, happy smile.*) Thank you, Kevin. But close the book now.

(HE does, slowly. Looks up at her. A beat.)

BOTH.
SOMEONE ELSE IS WAITING.
SOMEONE ELSE IS WANTING.
SOMEONE ELSE IS NEEDING
SOMEONE THERE TO HOLD.
SOMETHING ELSE IS SWEETER.
SOMETHING NEW CAN START.
NOT IN THE PLACE OF SOMETHING OLD:
NEWLY PLACED IN THE HEART.

NOLA.
BE IN LOVE AGAIN.

KEVIN. (*In musical echo.*)
(I'M IN LOVE RIGHT NOW.)

NOLA.
NEVER FEAR THAT HEARTS OFTEN BREAK.

KEVIN.
(NOT ANYMORE.)

NOLA.
LOVE IS WORTH THE RISK YOU TAKE ...

KEVIN.
(HEARTS ARE STRONGER THAN I THOUGHT.)

NOLA.
AND THE RE-CREATING.

KEVIN.
(AND I LOVE CREATING ...)

NOLA.
FIND YOUR JOY

AND YOUR PRIDE
IN THE ARMS
OPEN WIDE.

(A beat. SHE looks around one last time.)

YOUR ORDERLY WORLD IS BEAUTIFUL.

KEVIN.
NOW IT IS.

NOLA.
REALLY, KEVIN … BEAUTIFUL.

KEVIN. (*Meaning it at last.*)
I KNOW.

NOLA.
I'VE SEEN ENOUGH, THOUGH.

BOTH.
SOMEONE ELSE IS WAITING …

NOLA. Goodbye, Robert. I love you.

(And SHE disappears from the holo display. KEVIN stares into the pillar of light as though searching for some last trace of her; his reverie is interrupted by a buzz from the door to the lab. HE answers it … and the door slides open to reveal CAROL.)

CAROL. You called for a taxi, mister?

KEVIN. *(Looks confused, briefly, glancing at the holo display … then:*) I guess I did.

(HE starts to approach, when—
The holo chamber's doors open … to reveal JOHNNY BEAUMONT, singing "I Can Show You a Thing or Two." CAROL looks up, puzzled; KEVIN looks up toward the heavens and smiles. HE takes CAROL's hand in his, and, to her astonishment, starts to lead her in a dance.)

JOHNNY BEAUMONT.
I KNOW YOU GOT BURNED THE LAST TIME,
BUT THIS'LL BE TIME ANEW.
SO, BABY, IF YOU NEED RESCUE, I'M HERE
TO SHOW YOU A THING OR TWO ...!

(SHE leans her head against his shoulder and THEY dance — KEVIN moving with grace and feeling, as THEY share his — their *— orderly world. The dance becomes an embrace, and ...*
FADE OUT.)

CURTAIN

[MUSIC CUE # 25: BOWS]

PROPERTY PLOT

Directors and designers are encouraged to realize the physical aspects of *Weird Romance* in their own unique ways. Subsequently, the prop list that follows is not beholden to the original New York production. With few exceptions, it confines itself to the basic minimum required by the text. Ancillary props for creating mood, atmosphere, bits of business, etc. are up to the creative team behind each individual production.

The Girl Who Was Plugged In
Cigarettes
Beer can
Clipboard
Shopping bags
Trash can containing:
    Scarf
    White undershirt
    Styrofoam food tray
Two hand-held monitors
Hypospray
Breakfast (for Isham to offer P. Burke)
Picture or pictures (graphics) of Delphi
Thundercat Roberts contract
Binder with ad copy
Microphones
Reporter's camera
Easels with charts
Delphi's bracelet
Money (Paul gives to Bag Lady)
Pens
Delphi programs and/or Fan's autograph books

Her Pilgrim Soul
Boxing gloves (Boxer hologram)
Bouquet (Bride hologram)
Office paraphernalia for the lab:

- Yellow pads
- Clipboards
- Pens, etc.

Work paraphernalia for Carol and Rebecca:

- Post-its
- Paperwork
- Art supplies, etc.

Computer keyboard
Lab phone
Cordless phone (Carol)
Fetus
Paperwork: "The Matheson Layout" (Carol, Rebecca)
Copy of Nola's birth certificate
Stool (Nola)
Suitcase (Kevin)
Basket of laundry (Carol, Kevin)
Socks in basket
Steno pad (Daniel)
Pen (Daniel)
Flashlight (Chuck)
Trunk
Old photo scrapbook
Old-fashioned microphone on stand (Johnny Beaumont)
Abstract sculpture (possibly on stand)
Book of Yeats poetry

Note: One motif from the New York production that *is* recommended has to do with Nola's personal props. Since, as she matures, her age is implied, never stated, each new incarnation showed her with a single, but tellingly illustrative item. As a child, she had a doll. As a teenager, she had a book of poetry. As a young woman, she had needlepoint, etc. Though the selection of props may vary from production to production, the device itself is encouraged because it provides a terrific visual shorthand which may help both the actress and the production team to create immediate, visceral imagery for the audience to lock into.

A NOTE ABOUT SPECIAL EFFECTS, VISUALS and SETS or: IT'S ALL DONE WITH MIRRORS

Weird Romance was devised specifically to *seem* much more high-tech than it is. Primarily, it relies on common stage techniques, and the leaps of imagination are made in the audience's mind. For example, when consciousness shifts from P. Burke to Delphi in *The Girl Who Was Plugged In,* the illusion is created *entirely* by the actresses and the music. Supplementary support to such moments may be given by the director in league with his design team, though it is hardly mandatory and, in some instances, possibly ill-advised.

There are, however, a few illusions that *do* call for fairly simple design assistance. The solutions below were utilized in the original New York production; you may come up with your own.

HOLOGRAMS and the HOLO-CHAMBER

Anent the holo-chamber in *Her Pilgrim Soul* (Act II), it is important that the doors, when shut, completely conceal any playing areas to which the hologram figures may have access. For example, if there is a small stairway leading to the elevated platform serving as the floor of the chamber, and you wish Nola to make occasional use of it, *that stairway must be part of the enclosure.* The path of the doors describes the boundary beyond which the holograms cannot cross.

The "weird prismatic light" that makes the hologram actors "otherworldly and beautiful" in appearance can probably be created a number of ways. Our designers* did so by covering the floor of the holo-chamber with a

* Edward T. Gianfrancesco (sets) and Craig Evans (lighting)

layer of patterned, holographic filmcoated Mylar, inexpensively obtainable at (among, no doubt, other outlets) Industrial Plastics on Canal Street. (This "film" coating is also used to create the print hologram effects often displayed on book and magazine covers.) When hit with light of an intense enough power, the coated Mylar refracts the light into colors, much like a prism—but only at a 90° angle. The trick to using the material, then, is compensating for its bias. Therefore, the design team will have to experiment, according to the dimensions of the holo-chamber, with lighting instruments and Mylar shapes. (For example, in the New York production, bias compensation was achieved by cutting the Mylar into a sixteen-point star.) The effect is enhanced if the walls of the chamber are lined with patterned white tile onto which the prismatic light can be reflected; and if the costumes of all the hologram actors are primarily whites, off-whites and the lightest pastels: this helps create the illusion of their being ephemera (harder colors, unless used sparingly and selectively, will tend to "ground" the physical appearance of the actors, and make them seem too "real"). **Warning:** Proper ventilation—air-holes and a silent fan or two—*must* be designed into the holo-chamber if any effect like this is to be attempted, since the intense light creates a concomitant heat which, if it builds up, will make it hard for your actors to do basic things—such as staying conscious.

The fetus that appears gently floating in the holo-chamber can simply be a model, suspended by thin wires. As it appears and disappears on cue, it should be easy to rig and easy to remove—both silently.

SIMULACRA and the CYBER-CHAMBERS

In the original production of *The Girl Who Was Plugged In* (Act I), the left and right walls of the set were designed in gentle perspective, to keep them always in full view. The two cyber-chambers—human-sized enclosures—were built into the walls on mini-turntables. When they needed to be in view, they were; when the scene required that we leave GTX Control, the turntables were spun (manually), and the cyber-chambers disappeared.

The "bells and whistles" of *Weird Romance's* special effects are pretty much just that: bells and whistles. But to paraphrase Arthur C. Clarke—any sufficiently sophisticated use of stagecraft is indistinguishable from magic …

DAVID SPENCER's writing for the theatre also includes: the English adaptation and new lyrics for *La Boheme* at the Public Theatre; book and lyrics for The *Apprenticeship of Duddy Kravitz,* based on the novel by Mordecai Richler (music by Alan Menken); the music and lyrics for *Pulp,* a one act musical (book by Bruce Peyton) that has been produced in various regional venues as the most acclaimed segment of the anthology evening "Stories"; and *Playthings,* a one act play produced at Theatre Three in Los Angeles. In progress are: the lyrics for *Murder at the Vanities* (music by Donald Oliver, book by Donald E. Westlake), and the music and lyrics for a new musical, as yet untitled. In addition to writing scripts and stories for episodic television, Mr. Spencer has authored *Passing Fancy* an original novel based on the TV series *Alien Nation,* soon to be published by Simon & Schuster. He is on the faculty of the BMI-Lehman Engel Musical Theatre Workshop, and a member of the Dramatists Guild.

ALAN BRENNERT is a novelist and screenwriter whose books include *Time and Chance, Kindred Spirits,* and two collections of short fiction, *Her Pilgrim Soul and Other Stories* and *Ma Qui and Other Phantoms.* He has written for such television series as *China Beach, L.A. Law,* and *The Twilight Zone* (on which "Her Pilgrim Soul" first appeared, in an acclaimed production starring Anne Twomey and Kristoffer Tabori). Mr. Brennert won a 1991 Emmy Award for his work as a writer-producer on *L.A. Law,* and a Nebula Award, in 1992, for his short story "Ma Qui." He's also received three Writer's Guild Award nominations for outstanding teleplay of the year (in 1982 for *Darkroom,* in 1986 for "Her Pilgrim Soul," and in 1989 for *China Beach*), an Emmy nomination for best writing in a dramatic series (*L.A. Law*), and a Golden Globe nomination and People's Choice Award (for *L.A. Law*).

ALAN MENKEN composed the score and the songs for the current Disney animated film hit *Aladdin* (with lyricists Howard Ashman and Tim Rice). He is also responsible for composing the songs (with lyrics by Howard Ashman) and score for the enormously successful Disney animated film *Beauty and the Beast,* for which he received two Academy Awards as well as two Golden Globe Awards for Best Original Score and Best Song for the title song "Beauty and the Beast." For *The Little Mermaid*, Mr. Menken received two Academy Awards and two Golden Globe Awards for best score and best song ("Under the Sea") and two Grammy Awards. With lyricist Jack Feldman he has written "My Christmas Tree" for *Home Alone 2* and the songs for the musical feature *Newsies.*

With Howard Ashman, Mr. Menken received the New York Drama Critics Award, the Drama Desk Award, the Outer Critics Circle Award and the London Evening Standard Award for Best Musical for *Little Shop of Horrors* and an Oscar nomination for best song "Mean Green Mother From Outer Space" from the film version of *Little Shop*. In 1983, Mr. Menken received the BMI Career Achievement Award for a body of work for the musical theater including *Little Shop of Horrors; God Bless You, Mr. Rosewater; Real Life Funnies; Atina: Evil Queen of the Galaxy* (produced in workshop as *Battle of the Giants*); *Patch, Patch, Patch*; and contributions to numerous reviews including *Personals* and *Diamonds*. In 1987 a musical adaptation of *The Apprenticeship of Duddy Kravitz* with lyrics by David Spencer was produced in Philadelphia. Future musicals include *Kicks: The Showgirl Musical* with libretto by Tom Eyen. Mr. Menken wrote the score for the ABC miniseries *Lincoln* and also wrote the music and lyrics for the *Rocky V* theme song "The Measure of a Man" recorded by Elton John.

FAVORITE MUSICALS *from* "The House of Plays"

PHANTOM

(All Groups) Book by Arthur Kopit. Music & Lyrics by Maury Yeston. Large cast of m. & f. roles—doubling possible. Various Ints. & Exts. This sensational new version of Gaston Leroux' *The Phantom of the Opera* by the team which gave you *Nine* wowed audiences and critics alike with its beautiful music and lyrics, and expertly crafted book, which gives us more background information on beautiful Christine Daee and the mysterious Erik than even the original novel does. Christine is here an untrained street singer discovered by Count Philippe de Chandon, champagne tycoon. Erik, the Phantom of the Opera, is the illegitimate son of a dancer and the opera's manager. He becomes obsessed with the lovely Christine because her voice reminds him of his dead mother's. "Reminiscent of *The Hunchback of Notre Dame, Cyrano de Bergerac* and *The Elephant Man*, *Phantom*'s love story—and the passionately soaring music it prompts—are deliciously sentimental. Add Erik's father lovingly acknowledging his parenthood as his son is dying and the show jerks enough tears to fill that Paris Opera Lagoon."—San Diego Union. "Yeston and Kopit get us to care about the characters by telling us a lot about them, some of it funny, but most of it poignant."—Houston Chronicle. **(#18958)**

FAVORITE MUSICALS *from*

"The House of Plays"

A FINE AND PRIVATE PLACE

(All Groups) Book & Lyrics by Erik Haagensen. Music by Richard Isen. Adapted from the novel by Peter S. Beagle. 3m., 2f, (may be played by 2m., 2f.) + 1 raven (may be either m. or f.) Ext. setting. "The grave's a fine and private place,/But none, I think, do there embrace." Little did you know, Andrew Marvell, that someday, someone would come up with a charming love story, set in a graveyard, about two lost souls who are buried there, who meet and fall in love. Also inhabiting the cemetery is an eccentric old man who has the gift of being able to see and converse with the inhabitants of the graves, as well as with a raven who swoops in at mealtimes with some dinner he has swiped for the old guy. Also present from time to time is a delightful old Jewish widow, whose husband Morris is buried in the cemetery. She often stops by to tell Morris what's new. Her name is Gertrude, and it is soon apparent that she also stops by to flirt with old Jonathan Rebeck (she doesn't know he actually *lives* there). A crisis arises when it appears the young couple will be separated. The young man, it seems, has been deemed a suicide and, as such, he must be removed from consecrated ground. Their only hope is Jonathan; but to help them Jonathan must come out in the open. Had we but world enough, and time, we would tell you how Jonathan manages to salvage the romance; but we'll just have to hope the above story intrigues you enough to examine the delightful libretto and wonderfully tuneful music for yourself. A sell-out, smash hit at the Goodspeed in Connecticut and, later, at the American Stage Co. in New Jersey (the professional theatre which premiered *Other People's Money),* this happy, whimsical, sentimental, up-beat new show will delight audiences of all ages.. **(#8154)**

Other Publications for Your Interest

MAIL

(ADVANCED GROUPS—MUSICAL)

Book & Lyrics by JERRY COLKER
Music by MICHAEL RUPERS

9 men, 6 women—2 Sets

What a terrific idea for a "concept musical"! As *Mail* opens Alex, an unpublished novelist, is having an acute anxiety attack over his lack of success in writing and his indecision regarding his girlfriend, Dana; so, he "hits the ground running" and doesn't come back for 4 months! When Alex finally returns to his apartment, he finds an unending stream of messages on his answering machine and stacks and stacks of unopened mail. As he opens his mail, it in effect comes to life, as we learn what has been happening with Alex's friends, and with Dana, during his absence. There is also some hilarious junk mail, which bombards Alex muscially, as well as unpaid bills from the likes of the electric company (the ensemble comes dancing out of Alex's refrigerator singing "We're Gonna Turn Off Your Juice"). In the second act, we move into a sort of abstract vision of Alex's world, a blank piece of paper upon which he can, if he is able, and if he wishes, start over—with his writing, with his friends, with his father and, maybe, with Dana. Producers looking for something wild and crazy will, we know, want to open *this* MAIL, a hit with audiences and critics coast-to-coast, from the authors of THREE GUYS NAKED FROM THE WAIST DOWN! "At least 12 songs are solid enough to stand on their own. If MAIL can't deliver, there is little hope for the future of the musical theatre, unless we continue to rely on the British to take possession of a truly American art form."—Drama-Logue. "Make room for the theatre's newest musical geniuses."—The Same. (Terms quoted on application. Music available on rental. See p. 48.)

(#15199)

CHESS

(ADVANCED GROUPS—MUSICAL/OPERA)

Book by RICHARD NELSON
Lyrics by TIM RICE
Music by BJORN ULVAEUS & BENNY ANDERSSON

9 men, 2 women, 1 female child, plus ensemble

A *musical* about an *international chess match?!?!* A bad idea from the get-go, you'd think; but no—Tim Rice (he of *Evita*, *Joseph and the Amazing Technicolor Dreamcoat* and *Jesus Christ Superstar*), Bjorn Ulvaeus and Benny Andersson (they of Swedish Supergroup ABBA) and noted American playwright Richard Nelson, all in collaboration with Trevor Nunn (*Les Miz.*, *Nick Nick*, etc.) have pulled it off, creating an extraordinary rock opera about international intrigue which uses as a metaphor a media-drenched chess match between a loutish American champion (shades of Bobby Fischer) and a nice-guy Soviet champion. The American has a girlfriend, Florence, there in Bangkok (where the match takes place) to be his second and to provide moral support. There she meets, and falls in love with, Anatoly, the Soviet champion—and the sparks fly, particularly when Anatoly decides to defect to the west, causing a postponement and change of venue to Budapest. Eventually, it is clear that all the characters are merely pawns in a larger chess match between the C.I.A. and the KGB! The pivotal role of Florence is perhaps the most extraordinary and complex role in the musical theatre since Eva Peron; and the roles of Freddie and Anatoly (both tenors) are great, too. Several of the songs have become international hits, including Florence's "Heaven Help My Heart", "I know Him So Well" and "Nobody's On Nobody's Side", and Freddie's descent into the maelstrom of decadence, "One Night in Bangkok". Playing to full houses and standing ovations, *Chess* closed exceedingly prematurely on Broadway; and, perhaps the story behind *that* just might make the basis of another Rice/ABBA/Nelson/Nunn collaboration! (Terms quoted on application. Music available on rental. See p. 48.) Slightly restricted.

(#5236)